A Bend in Time

A Bend in Time

Tales from la Savoie

PAS de Vrai

Cœur de Rose Publishing

CONTENTS

DEDICATIONS   vii
COPYRIGHT   ix
OTHER BOOKS   xi

1 | Introduction to a Bend in Time   1

2 | A Bend in Time   6

3 | Love in the Sierroz   23

4 | The Village of Pluvis   37

5 | The Face in the Curtain   55

6 | The Bat Cave   80

7 | The Land of Four Half Elephants   113

I would like to dedicate this first work of fiction to my many friends in France and especially to those living within the beautiful and ancient Duchy of Savoie; you know who you are and the deep affection I hold for you!

Also available from Cœur de Rose Publishing

By Malcolm Marks (author) in the Itinerant Ecologist Series:

1. 'From Nigeria to Cracking Walnuts' (2023)

   Available in hard copy (ISBN: 978-2-9590283-0-4)
   and electronic version (ISBN: 978-2-9590283-1-1)

2. 'There's a Crocodile in the House' (2023)

   Available in hard copy (ISBN: 978-2-9590283-2-8)
   and electronic version (ISBN: 978-2-9590283-3-5)

3. 'Sapphires, Monkey-Bread and a *Coup d'Etat*' (2024)

   Available in hard copy (ISBN: 978-2-9590283-4-2)
   and electronic version (ISBN: 978-2-9590283-5-9)

4. 'Of Cows, Chars and Beautiful People'
   (in preparation)

Introduction to a Bend in Time

The beautiful and historic region of Savoy or la Savoie abounds with legends and myths and possesses a proud local population who, while French, are proudest to be known as the Savoyards.

La Savoie was not always a part of France indeed it was once an important Duchy in its own right holding lands not only in Savoie but also southwards to Nice. To the east it possessed parts of mainland Italy together with Sicily and later Sardinia. From 1416 to 1563, the capital of the Duchy was Chambery before it moved to Turin where it remained until 1713.

In 1860 its French territories were annexed by France under the Treaty of Turin and they remain an integral part of France to the present day. At the same time, the last Duke of Savoie became the King of Italy while the very last King of Italy, Umberto II, was interred in the imposing Hautecombe Abbey in 1983. Hautecombe sits on the banks of the beautiful Lac du Bourget and opposite the important bath town of Aix-les-Bains. A town where Queen Victoria and her daughter Eugenie were frequent visitors 'to take the waters' in the late 1800s.

Gossip tells that Queen Victoria was so mean with the heating of Buckingham Palace that the poor Princess Eugenie suffered terribly from arthritis and so came to Aix for the annual 'Cure'.

Often forgotten is that Ain, the department immediately to the west of Savoie, was also once an integral part of the Duchy. It appears that settlements controlled by Counts of Savoie began to appear in the department back in the eleventh century and in 1355 much of the East bank of the Rhone was a part of the Duchy of Savoie. By the fifteenth century much of modern day Ain belonged to Savoie and remained an integral part until 1601 when Henri IV of France conquered the territory of Ain and it became a part of the Duchy of Burgundy.

The old French territories of the Duchy are fascinating places rich, not only in history but also in folklore. The folklore has been bred out of the natural beauty of the area where exist the highest mountains, the deepest and largest natural lakes and the densest of forests on steep scarp slopes. Is it so surprising that our folklore is so rich? I think not.

This series of short stories includes two that come directly from local and ancient folklore but of course painted with my own personal brush. The first is the tale of Ondine, a beautiful lovesick creature who finally caught her handsome lover, Pierre. The setting for the story is the mischievous River Sierroz and, if you walk the banks of the river, you can still find most of the settings for the story. If you do, you will certainly fall under its charm - but beware of Ondine because you might be the next on her list!

The second local myth is the story of the Lac de Pluvis which, until recent times, lay close to the River Rhone. The lake appeared suddenly one dark rainy winter's night and swallowed up the small and unfriendly village of the same name. The *Grotte de la Bonne*

Femme, where part of the story is set, exists to this day and is well worth a visit.

Two more of the stories are developed from tales that I was told as recently as the 1990s. The first about the assassination of poor Pascalino, a simple farm labourer who fell for the charms of his employer's wife, is based on a story that continues to do the rounds in local villages. The second, about the discovery of a beautiful cave system above a magnificent waterfall is based on a true story and, indeed, I visited the cave with my two children many years ago and saw the skeleton of a dog lying on a shelf of soil.

The final two stories will be thought by most to be pure fiction ... but are they really? I developed the idea for 'The Bend in Time' as I drove from Yenne towards and then through the Tunnel du Chat, eventually appearing on the promontory overlooking the magnificent Lac du Bourget. The view of the lake in front of the tunnel exit and the often snow-covered Alps to the south must be one of France's most amazing panoramas.

The final story about Alioune, Mi-Mi and Matar as they make their way from the Peanut Basin in Senegal to Chambery is a work of complete fiction although a lot of the details are based on my extended stays in that sahelian country.

I hope that this extract will have given you a taster of their young adventures as I am developing their story into a full length book that is to be published by Cœur de Rose Publishing in the not too distant future.

But while I state honestly that this final work is complete fiction, as I was researching and writing the story, I could not help ask myself how the hundreds of thousands of migrants who cross into Europe every year manage to arrive at their crossing points with their funds still intact. My logic (perhaps flawed) says that if a crossing costs several thousand euros in cash per person, would not the aspiring immigrants simply be robbed of their possessions and money as they trekked through North Africa or Syria and Turkey; indeed long before they could arrive at their embarkation points? How then do so many migrants arrive at crossing points on the coast or on the borders of eastern Europe with sufficient funds available to pay their passages? Puzzling. Or could it be, as the story suggests, that organisations (let's call them what they are 'businesses') exist that demand a period of near slave labour as the price of a crossing? And are those organisations in contact, working in complicity, with the Action Warriors and the Action Italias of this world? We know such humanitarian associations exist, indeed some are even funded with French taxpayers' money pertaining to be donations from some of our largest cities. Those cities are in turn strong magnets for the illegal immigrants who manage to make their hazardous journeys to our country every year.

Furthermore, every tourist town, every local flea market, every coast has its own Alioune and Matar who set up shop during the summer months on lengths of material placed on the pavements and sell 'genuine fakes' to kids who do not care that their designer sunglasses at ten euros are bad imitations of the real thing.

Try saying 'na-ga-def' (how are you?) to these traders and, I assure you, they will happily reply to you in Wolof. Most of them do actually come from the Peanut Basin and many are members of the Brotherhood. Ask them how they made their journeys from the Land of Teranga to la Belle France. Their replies will be well worth the cost of buying one of their 'genuine fakes'.

I hope you enjoy reading this first book of my 'Tales from la Savoie'. I am always collecting suitable stories and legends, there are so many out there to be heard and interpreted. I will be publishing more in the not too distant future.

P-A S de Vrai
March 2024

2

A Bend in Time

4th July, 2023: I am writing down my story in case someone, at some time, any time, finds my computer. Please pass it on to the senior journalist at the X-Times Newspaper. He is my friend and will know what to make of my story. To ease access to the computer's contents, I have removed my official password and encryption software ensuring that my files can be readily accessed. I know I do not have a great deal of time left to me; what an enigma I find myself trapped in; you will see.

My name is Georges, Georges Eiffel. Yes, just like the tower in Paris. Family lore even has it that we are descended from Gustave but since no-one has bothered to trace back our genealogy, I expect that now I will never know. And anyway, that is irrelevant to my current plight.

I am 54 years old, born in the year 1969, a nuclear engineer. I work (or at least I did when I left my laboratory after lunch today) for the International Centre for Nuclear Research.

You have never heard of that organisation? Don't worry, not many people have because it is rated above top secret. ICNR is a cross-border research institute buried deep in the Jura mountains between France and Switzerland. It is funded by a mix of friendly national governments, cash-loaded multinationals and a few discrete as well as famous individuals; all very rich.

ICNR is a military-oriented offshoot of the better known European nuclear facility. Most of our staff were recruited from that sister institute; attracted not only by far higher salaries but also the scientific chance to work on the unthinkable.

The activities of my team are no different. We are doing the unthinkable too. Our work is fascinating, challenging – and, I should say no more, at least while I am still alive. Then, I will let my computer do my talking. After my death, the Official Secrets Order that I signed at recruitment will become null and void; anyway what can the managing authorities do to me once I am deceased?

Let me tell you my story:

Today, July 4th 2023 – coincidentally US Independence Day – started out as any ordinary day, absolutely no different from so many others. As usual, I awoke to a clamouring alarm clock (I don't naturally 'do early') in my chalet home in a small village called Saint-Claude that lies well within the Jura Regional National Park. The house is not owned by me but by the ICNR. Indeed, all scientists of my pay grade are housed for free on the institute's private estate and all our bills are covered by them. We are twenty-two seniors who live in close proximity to each other. None of us receives mail or bills or any other form of outside communications because knowledge of our presence in the national park lies outside the public domain. This is to protect us and, by so doing, protect our work and therefore the ICNR itself. To neighbours, friends, family and indeed to the heavy bureaucracies of France and Switzerland, my official residence is in Aix-les-Bains; a stone's throw from the beautiful *Lac du*

Bourget where my wife and two teenage twin children live and carry on their lives as any other *famille Aixoise.*

I left the office just after lunchtime today, far earlier than usual because I have some accumulated holiday time to enjoy. The distance between my workplace and home is around 130 kilometres, and the drive usually takes about two hours, that is, if I do not bother the speed cameras at various points along my route. But today the drive was to have been a little longer because I had a shopping list of items to purchase and so needed to deviate a few kilometres off my usual route.

First I stopped in *Jongieux* where I picked up a large case of the dry white *Savoie* wine that my wife loves so much, and then on to *Saint-Jean-de-Chevelu* to collect our telephoned order of fruit and vegetables from the roadside stand manned, or I should say, lady'ed by Florence.

By the time I had finished a long chat at the vineyard, and another with Jean-Patrick at the fruit stand, my car clock was show-ing 4.30 pm. As I set out from chez-Florence, I remember thinking that I should be home in twenty minutes max, just about in time to welcome my seventeen-year-old twins, Lilith and Nathan, home from *Lycée*. Little did I know.

I drove up the rather steep hill that took me away from St-Pierre-de-Chevelu, past the roundabout with its cute sculpture of a bicycle erected for a past Tour de France, on to the winding approach for the '*Tunnel du Chat*' and then around the tunnel's roundabout. All seemed normal.

I entered the tunnel, hearing the family clunk, clunk, clunk of the three poorly sealed manhole covers at the entrance, just about respecting the 50 km per hour speed limit, and noticed that the road was very quiet this afternoon; not another vehicle in sight.

But I knew that only 1,500 metres away awaited one of France's most beautiful sights.

The first part of the tunnel through the mountain that overlooks the *Lac du Bourget* describes a gentle uphill slope and, as I crested the brow of the incline, I saw without really seeing a double flash of light. My subconscious mind put those flashes down to the brilliant sunlight showing at the far end of the tunnel; any rational mind would. That was my mistake, sadly it would soon prove that it was not what I had originally thought.

As I continued to drive through the tunnel, I began to daydream about the coming few days' vacation that we would spend *en famille*. First, I had promised to take the twins out on Joaquim's boat to see if we could tempt a few Alpine Char on to our hooks. In Aix we call these fish *lavaret* but my Swiss colleagues insist their name is *féra,* but no matter. And in the evening, after the fishing expedition, I planned a romantic evening at a little restaurant we love, just set back from the lakeside at the Grand Port called *Le Riva*. Sophie and Cyrille are the owners, waitress and chef and just about the nicest couple managing a restaurant across the whole of Aix.

As I snapped out of the daydream, that I suppose must have lasted a minute or so, I realised that I was no nearer to the tunnel exit than when the daydream began. Odd. My mind immediately starts one of its mathematical calculations that it so loves to do:

If the tunnel is 1,500 metres long and I am driving at 50 km per hour, how far would I travel during, say, a one-minute daydream? Well at 60 km per hour the calculation is easier because a kilometre (or a 1,000 metres) is knocked off in precisely a minute, obviously a little less distance is covered at a speed of 50. But a minute is plenty of time at 50 km per hour to cover the entire remaining 800 or so metres of the tunnel that remained after I had crested the brow of the incline. So, how come I have not yet reached the end?

I drove on, telling myself to concentrate but it really seemed as though I was getting no closer to the tunnel's exit; indeed, I had not even reached the next maintenance door that crop up every few hundred metres. What is happening?

What would you do in such a situation? Well, I did just the same. I shook my head and told myself to wake up. But even after that I really was getting no nearer to the end of the tunnel.

I then decided to count slowly and out loud to 100 using the old timing device of 'one Kodak, two Kodak, three Kodak' and so on. I told myself that that should represent close to two minutes of time, but it was probably far more. When I finally arrived at one hundred Kodak I found I was still no closer to the tunnel exit. Even watching the yellow lights on the nearside wall, interspersed after each four with a blue light, bought me no closer to leaving the tunnel.

Then, at that very precise moment when I spoke out loud the last 100 Kodak, those two bright flashes came back to the front of my mind, and I cursed loudly. It was precisely then that the first inklings of my dire predicament began to dawn on me.

Perhaps now I should start to explain what my work at ICNR involves.

While we, the scientist, are fascinated by our work on a purely scientific discovery level – and I believe that fascination is shared by the rich private philanthropists who help finance us – it is an open secret within the staff at ICNR that our 'far beyond the frontiers of science' activities are viewed on a predominantly military basis by the governments that fund us.

At its simplest, my work centres on time and space. Imagine that we could be inside a bubble where time appears to continue at its normal pace while outside the bubble time almost stops. Imagine that a year, two years, ten years can pass within the bubble but it only represents a heartbeat outside. Well, discovering how to create that bubble is the thrust of my work and, two days ago, my team and I succeeded for the first time in achieving that ambition.

How is that possible, I hear you ask? Obviously the detailed answer would be rather complicated to explain to the layman! But I can try to explain it with a couple of simple analogies with which most people will be familiar.

I know that most people will have heard about the theory of wormhole travel; Star Trek was an incredible series for popularising complex ideas like wormhole travel, the warp-drive and the deatomising transporter (as in 'Beam me up Scotty' a phrase that Captain Kurt apparently never uttered). In wormhole travel, our understanding of physical laws, brings us to believe that we should be able to move very rapidly through time and space. The theory says that ordinarily we travel through time and space as if we are on a flat piece of paper and that is why it takes such a long time, light years in fact, to travel to other places around the universe. However, the theory goes on to say that at certain places in the universe or with sufficient energy, the paper is (or can be made to become) folded allowing us, theoretically of course, to pop down the wormhole and arrive quickly at a point far away in space. Sadly, we are far, far away from wormhole travel simply because of the enormous energy that is required to generate the wormhole and then to survive the travel through it.

Now, as for my work, imagine the reverse situation. Imagine that our usual time – as the hands of our clock move around its face – and our space – all around us as we move from place to place – already passes along a form of natural wormhole.

Do you see? If we turn the wormhole theory around and imagine instead that we can create the opposite effect to wormhole travel. Imagine that while our daily lives move through a permanent wormhole, we are able to step out of the hole and on to the flat sheet of paper. In order to arrive at the same place in space and time as we would in our normal lives, we must now move much faster (or normal life must *seem* to slow right down).

Can you see that as we move out of our normal wormhole and onto the sheet of paper that we would now need far longer and would travel much further to go from A to B than would be the case as we move – as we do all day – along natural wormhole pathways? Complicated to grasp that idea, I agree!

So, perhaps my second analogy to explain our discovery around time, distance and space is simpler to follow. Consider then the speed of the current in a meandering river. Did you know that the water on the outside curve of a river moves more quickly than the water on the inside curve? Yup, I promise you, it really does! That's why rivers drop sediment on the slower-moving inside bend while eroding the banks on the faster moving outer side.

Now take that analogy to time inside nature's wormholes compared to time on the sheet of paper. While our normal time and space can be considered as following the inside of the meander, and is therefore slower, if we move to the outside of the curve, time would need to speed up relative to the normal speed on the inside.

This, of course, all beggars the question of what we have been able to achieve. Currently, we have gone as far as to create a time-space bubble with everything inside the bubble moving at the accelerated pace while all outside the bubble proceeds at life's normal speed. Or turn that around, and what appears the normal speed inside the bubble, represents almost nothing outside. As I mentioned earlier, a year in the bubble might be a mere heartbeat in normal time. And the beauty of our system? It requires almost no energy; in fact the inverse of creating a wormhole or travelling down it. Indeed, we used a simple lithium battery – as people have inside their cell phones – to generate our first time-space bubble in the laboratory. Yes, the very opposite energy requirement to theorised wormhole travel.

In our laboratory experiment, we were able to generate our first space-time bubble measuring about sixteen square metres (the size of a decent sitting room) around a pair of young rats that were provided with several large canisters containing food and water. We timed the experiment to last ten seconds of our time and when that time had passed, we were astonished to find some three hundred mummified corpses and all canisters of food and water completely empty. Carbon-14 dating of the mummified corpses showed them to be several hundred years old; all that in ten seconds of our usual time!

Back to my current situation, somehow a time-space bubble has been created around me, exactly how I do not know. Perhaps one of my junior colleagues wanted to continue testing our system and is trying out another ten-second run. Ten seconds of your time is nothing, after all, but for me inside the bubble, such a test will last more than three hundred years. I think now that the reader may well understand why I do not hold out much hope of coming out of this adventure intact. Even if my colleague does a rapid switch on and off, that could well represent a year or more of my time inside the bubble; I simply do not have the resources to survive that long.

Day two Inside the Bubble (IB2) – I have spent the last twenty-four hours coming to terms with my predicament and analysing my situation. The first thing that I realised is that there is no night and day inside the bubble; I got trapped in the bubble in daylight and so it will be daylight during my whole period of captivity. However, (do not ask me how), the numbers of my digital car clock and the hands of my wristwatch continue their normal (to me that is) progression and so I can judge time within my time-space prison.

I have paced out my bubble and find that it covers an area of approximately twelve metres down the tunnel but only ten metres across it. The rest of the circular bubble must be inside the limestone rock of the mountain and so obviously I have no access to that additional area. But that still gives me around one hundred squares metres of living space. Luck is on my side in another respect too (can I *really* talk about luck?) because the bubble includes one of the escape cum maintenance areas that sits behind a door. Guess where my toilet is going to be.

One big decision I made during my analysis is to try to follow the motto of "Where there is life, there is hope" and so I intend to stay alive for as long as possible; I doubt it will be very long given my small stock of food but I owe it to my lovely wife and the twins not to give up hope.

The entire stock of food that I possess is composed of just one shopping bag of fruit and another of vegetables plus a case of a dozen bottles of white wine, *vins de Savoie*. My Swiss army knife, proves yet again that everyone should have one since it has a corkscrew! In the glove compartment we always keep a sharp *Opinel* (what Frenchman doesn't?) that goes with me on my frequent wild mushroom hunting trips or serves to cut *saucissons* during occasional picnics with the twins. And, oh yes, I have noticed a box of extra strong tic-tacs that madam loves to crunch while driving.

But, even more important to sustaining life, my life that is, I have located within my time-space bubble, a section of the tunnel wall where there is a steady drip of water that has found its way through natural fissures in the limestone rocks above and is dripping down through a crack in the cement and tiles that line the tunnel. My empty Costa coffee cup is now placed under the drip and so, for the moment at least, I have water to drink, sort of on tap …

I have made the decision to keep my computer alive for as long as possible by periodically plugging it into the cigarette lighter port of my car. Of course, this will slowly run down the car battery but I anticipate that I can keep the computer powered up for about a couple of months. Plenty of time for me to write my story, work out a strategy for staying alive as long as possible, and to develop a diary that I anticipate our local X-Times newspaper will certainly wish to publish.

After all these positives, I have found that sadly I cannot increase the longevity of my car battery by occasionally running the petrol engine because when I tried, I realised that my bubble retains almost all its air and so I risk killing myself more rapidly through simple carbon monoxide poisoning than accelerated time will likely eventually achieve!

Day three Inside the Bubble (IB3) – Apart from continuing to write my diary, I find that I have little to do while trapped here. So my thoughts have turned to survival or rather how I can try to extend my life expectancy as far into the future as possible. One of my activities has been to sort through the two bags of fruit and vegetables purchased chez Florence and to divide the contents into three piles.

The first pile contains food that will quickly perish: a bag of juicy peaches, freshly arrived from *La Drôme*, a box of strawberries from a local farmer, two very crisp Batavia lettuces, and six avocadoes from southern Spain that were on special offer as they were already ripe to eat. I calculate that I can only keep these for a maximum of ten days and so they will serve as my immediate food source.

The second pile contains food that should be able to last for up to a month and in this pile I have placed a kilogram of slightly unripe tomatoes, four sweet peppers and three aubergines, and a bunch of spicy radishes. There is also a large bunch of very unripe bananas.

The third and final pile contains three kilos of potatoes, a kilo of green beans, a kilo of onions, a bunch of shallots and three full bulbs of garlic, a kilo of leeks and another kilo of turnips. Not much fun in eating that lot raw (and luckily there is no one else in here with me!). I believe that in the cool conditions close to the middle of the tunnel, my final pile may well stretch my food – and indigestion – to around two months.

Of course, the item that should last the longest is the eleven bottles of white wine. What's that I hear? "twelve," you say? Oh, I forgot to mention that I went on a bender during my first night alone and sucked down a whole bottle. It was the hangover of the following morning that almost convinced me that life was not worth living but two paracetamols washed down by generous swallows of lime-loaded tunnel water brought back my resilience!

IB7 – and I have now realised that my ambition to stretch my food over at least two months was flawed. Although it is far cooler in the middle of the *Tunnel du Chat* than it is outside in the beautiful July weather we have come to expect in Aix-les-Bains, my car computer still tells me that the temperature in the bowels of the earth is holding at 24C, plenty high enough for mould to start to spread across several of the fruit still remaining in the first pile, and I am concerned that some of my second pile will soon become infected. What to do to ensure that my available food gets to last a little longer?

After wracking my rather fuddled brain, I have come up with an idea. While living and working in Senegal, I had been shown by Senegalese friends how the water in local earthenware pots – or *canari* as they call them – can be considerably cooler than the ambient temperature. How does that work? Well, the earthenware pots are slightly porous and so water slowly soaks through to the outside and then evaporates. The process of evaporation requires energy (heat) and that energy comes partly from the mass of water itself thus cooling it down. Now, as surprising as it may seem, I do not carry an earthenware pot from Senegal around with me in the car. However, what I do have is a small suitcase, the type we are allowed to take onboard a Ryan Air flight. This I empty of my clothes, stack smaller items around the edges (to act as insulation) place my more delicate fruit and vegetables inside, lay an old pullover plus a small towel over the top, trying not to touch the food beneath, and douse these liberally with water that I have been collecting in my Costa coffee cup. I hope that evaporation from the pullover and towel will do the trick of reducing the temperature inside the suitcase by a few degrees and thus preserve my meagre stock of food for a few extra days. Time will tell (excuse the pun), and I have plenty of that. A small breeze conveniently blows close to the surface of the road, helping the water in my woollen jumper to slowly evaporate.

IB14 – another issue with my food has appeared. This morning I find my two remaining, and now very soggy, peaches have somehow bred a colony of tiny maggots. Not the thick white ones that the twins use as fish bait when we go to catch trout in the lake at Saint-Jean-de-Chevelu but small, thin and very wiggly ones. Nothing ventured, nothing gained ... down the hatch they go for a little bit of protein; the first protein since I got stuck in my time-space bubble!

And swallowing those tiny maggots gives me another idea: what if I search out other invertebrate life that has got stuck in my bubble along with me? After all, in my one hundred or so square metres there must be a few arthropods and other insects around. I start a search, carrying the paper bag that had contained my garlic bulbs in readiness. I consider that the obvious place to find flies, spiders, woodlice and their ilk must be where there is water. I walk over to my coffee cup that is catching the persistent drips from the wall, and start my search. Absolutely nothing. That is a bit depressing and I decide to drown my sorrows with a few glasses (read swigs) of white wine. Laying across my makeshift bed on the backseat of the car I slowly savour the *Savoie* wine while chewing on a raw potato. I reflect on how nice it would be to have something other than carbohydrate to eat; but no chance of that it seems.

I sit up to swig a last mouthful of wine and say out loud "oh derr Georges Eiffel!"

Carefully placing the bottle down on the pavement outside the car, I go over to my suitcase cum refrigerator, lift it up and there between the bottom of the case and the road surface in the shade, cool, darkness and humidity sits my evening meal: two small slugs and a tiny earthworm. I have just learnt the secret of hunting some local wildlife!

I can imagine anyone that will be reading my ramblings (you would ramble too if you were sentenced to spend an unknown amount of time in solitary confinement) will ask themselves "how can this idiot possibly eat slugs?"

Well, the story goes back to when I was about seven years old and my *papy* (grandfather) explained to me that since people in France like to eat snails, he could see no valid reason why we should not also be able to eat slugs, *n'est-ce pas mon petit*? He went on to explain that the only difference between a slug and a snail was that the former was homeless. To a seven-year old that made a lot of sense and for several months after he told me that story, I naively imagined that slugs wandered around the garden simply searching for an empty shell not looking for juicy lettuces!

As we sat around our little campfire on the hillside of his idyllic home in the little town of Crémieu where, coincidentally, we were boiling potatoes in an upturned World War One German helmet (I exaggerate not, such are the perfect memories I have of my *papy*), he picked up a long, orange slug and laid it sizzling on to one of the rocks that he had carefully placed to enclose our fire.

When he was sure that it was well cooked, he took out his *Opinel* and sliced it along its back, telling me "creatures without backbones, like slugs, are strange beings because their stomach and intestines run along their backs. We need to remove them before eating because we do not know what they might contain."

"You mean like poo, *papy*?" I queried.

"Well, yes, if you want to put it like that but really, slugs and snails are able to eat many plants that are poisonous to us, so better to take out their guts first; you never know what it had for its last meal!" He then proceeded to cut the slug in two, and popped the head end into his mouth and chewed appreciatively. I followed suit with the rest!

Now, the observant reader will be thinking that eating a well-cooked slug is one thing but a raw slug? Yuk!

Ah, but 'where there's a will, there is most certainly a way'. My car has one of those thingamajigs for lighting cigarettes and so I can cook my slugs, remove the innards and down the hatch they go chased by a swig of wine. No chewing, I will allow my digestive juices and stomach acids to sort them out, but at least I get some more protein.

IB31 – today I am celebrating a month in my prison. I have stopped thinking of what a brilliant scientist I am to have created the Time-Space Bubble with my team. Rather I feel (and most certainly look) like a destitute. My beard has grown, well sort of, since by looking in the rear view mirror I can see that it appears rather moth-eaten in two or three places where whiskers have always stubbornly refused to grow. I also have one patch to the side of my mouth which is starkly white while the rest of the beard is dark and healthy looking. I laugh out loud thinking that I have achieved a growth that closely resembles that of a certain famous politician hailing from one of our northern ports.

I am only too aware that my food is starting to run out. I only have a couple of potatoes, a turnip and one leek left. I have ditched the idea of chewing raw garlic and instead have managed to press drops of garlic juice with the flat blade of my *Opinel* into my drinking water. That way I am getting the goodness of the vegetable without the accompanying and severe indigestion!

But I have to make a confession to you: I feel my survival resolve is sliding away. This is accompanied by strange sleep patterns. Sometimes, I am unable to sleep for several days in a row and then I fall into a dreamless state that can go on for fourteen or fifteen hours at a time. I know this is a symptom of slow starvation and lack of the correct balance of essential vitamins and minerals. I have been spending considerable amounts of my free time – and that's all I have plenty of – looking for anything to eat that might help rebalance my diet. But apart the occasional small beetle, I am finding less and less insects, worms and slugs every day; not surprising.

IB40 – I have no food left. I still have water to drink and there still remain four unopened bottles of wine. I have been rationing my tic-tacs to one a day and there are two left in the container. But I can no longer drink the wine 'neat' as it causes me soon to become drunk and rapidly and very violently sick. Nor can I suck on the remaining tic-tacs as the peppermint hurts my stomach too much. What I am doing is to add some of wine and a tic-tac to my water cup and allow the alcohol to become very diluted and the sweets to melt. But I know that I am now only stretching out the inevitable conclusion to my life.

Let's be honest, I have been malnourished for about fifteen days already and, from this moment on, I am entering a period of real starvation. My ever more fuddled brain tells me that in the absence of food but with access to water, I can probably remain alive for another twenty-five to thirty days. That's the good news. The bad news is that I am going to become increasingly weak and less able to leave the comfort of my car and get to my cup to drink the water it is still catching.

What does this mean? It means that at some time soon, I must leave my car and set up a bed within reach of my cup. Better to do that now than wait and risk become too weak to move.

IB47 – I awake with a start from my dream of a herd of sheep grazing in a field. My mind is not clear. It is trying to tell me that I have forgotten something; something to do with the car. What on earth?

I lay there trying to think what the issue can be. And then, all at once, the clouds start to lift from my confused mind. I softly swear because I have suddenly realised that when I moved my bed out of the car and next to the water source, I had forgotten to plug my computer in to recharge from the car battery.

"Does it really matter?" I ask myself, "well, yes, it does" is the response my mind gives me.

I crawl lethargically towards the car door on my stomach and pull myself with heavy arms and push with weighted legs until I am laying across the passenger seat and able to grab the jack plug to try to insert it back into the lighter socket. But too late, the computer dies two seconds before I can plug it back in.

At the very moment that my fuddled brain is thinking 'blast I will now have to go through the entire boot-up process' I simultaneously see a double flash of light and hear cars zooming towards me.

3

Love in the Sierroz

My name is Ondine and I live in the valley of the petulant Sierroz River that takes its source in the little commune of Montcel in Savoie. Our river starts off as a mere trickle but then races almost twenty kilometres, first north and then east, dropping more than eight hundred metres in the process until it finally plunges and becomes lost in the placid but deep and mysterious waters of the Lac du Bourget.

The area of the Sierroz where I live is both beautiful and quiet, if a little wild and rugged. My home lies just downstream from the ruins of the Dalby Mill that once used the rapid passage of the river to turn its large wooden wheel that set in motion the grinding of the millstones for the production of flour.

Before you read my story, and perhaps then you will not judge me too harshly, I have to confess that I have always been deeply in love with Pierre, the miller's handsome son. You should also know that we knew each other for almost two decades before the final events of my story occur. I first met Pierre by the river bank when he was only three years old. On our first meeting he was with his mother, a pretty but tired looking young woman who helped her husband Tom at a time when the mill was still active.

She brought little Pierre to the riverbank not only so that he could play but also to teach him, at such an early age, about the dangers of the waters that flow so rapidly in our river. That was the first moment that we met and when my affections for him began to form. At least, at that age, I thought he was cute! Those affections would later grow to such an intensity that I knew I could not exist without him in my life.

At such a tender age, he had walked hesitantly down the steep path that led from the footpath at the top of the Sierroz's gully to the riverside. His mother led the way down the path carefully gripping small trees and shrubs with her left hand as she descended and holding her right hand behind her so that Pierre could grip it tightly with his left. In his other hand, I saw that he clutched a small wooden boat with a tiny sail, made of red cloth divided into four quarters by a white cross – our noble flag of la Savoie.

I was already at the bottom of the path and whispered '*bonjour*' as he approached. Pierre smiled after I spoke, so clearly he heard me but I think he was perhaps rather too shy to respond.

I watched as he put his little boat into the water and I could not help smiling as I saw how tightly he held the loop tied to the length of string that was attached to a small hook at the rear; perhaps I should say 'stern', of his boat. As soon as the boat was launched, the Sierroz whisked it away from the bank and little Pierre shrieked with pleasure as it progressed out into the current and then moved rapidly downstream. However, once the string was stretched to its limit, the little boat began to move rapidly towards the bank where I helped to guide it back upstream towards him, marvelling as I saw the small breeze, that often blows along the gully of the Sierroz, fill the sail and complete my work of returning the boat to the shore.

Pierre's mum held his hand tightly while he picked the little boat out of the more placid waters at the bank's edge and repeated, several times, the launching and retrieval processes. Thus began for Pierre a lifetime of love for the Sierroz and everything to do with boats.

Of course, a little boy's attention span is limited and soon he moved on to trying to skip stones in the calm pool that lies just off the bank. The first five or six stones he selected simply made a plop and sunk without trace but his mother proved quite adept at stone skipping and showed Pierre how to choose the flattest among the stones and then to throw them with an arm movement that kept the stone parallel with the water. Soon Pierre had learnt the trick and his laughter rang out as he achieved his first bouncing stone. Bless him.

That initial afternoon together proved to be the first of many over innumerable years. Regardless of the season, we would always seek each other out at this place at the bottom of the steep path, our place, on the Sierroz. But, until he had learnt to swim strongly – an obligation for any child living near water – he was always accompanied by his mum, and occasionally also by his dad.

As he grew we interacted more and more and, by the time he was ten and a strong swimmer (at least in the calm but surprisingly deep waters of the *Lac du Bourget*), he would come to visit me on his own. We spoke little, preferring simply to enjoy each other's company. I tended to idle the time away splashing near the bank while Pierre often brought a length of bamboo that he had fashioned into a fishing rod and tried to tempt the fat rainbow trout that abounded in the faster waters of the river with an earthworm or a large white maggot that he found in rotting tree stumps that he had kicked over.

By the age of thirteen, Pierre was beginning to become a very handsome young man with a croaking voice that appeared to be linked to a lengthening of his chin. But, before reaching his thirteenth birthday, indeed a year previously, he was obliged to leave school in order to help his father in the mill. I realised with sadness, that we would likely see each other rather less because of his work obligations in the mill.

Leaving school was not a pleasant experience for Pierre. Not only was he a bright young man able to read, write and use mathematics and thus well suited to go on to become a clerk or even a teacher; if only his dad did not need him to help in the mill. But also his poor mum was heavily pregnant with her third child and had been unable to help in the mill for several months already. There was no option for Pierre's dad but to insist that Pierre leave school and work in the mill with him.

In October of that year, Pierre's mum went into labour. Pierre was dispatched by his dad to bring the midwife or '*la sage femme*' from the village. The sage femme was a rotund lady of advancing years that had, in their time, delivered not only Pierre and his younger brother, Patrick, but also Pierre's mum and his dad.

Luckily the old lady was at home drinking a steaming cup of chicory when Pierre came bursting through her front door panting hard and trying to catch his breath after the race across the fields and uphill from the mill to the village.

"*Calmes-toi, mon petit*" said the old lady. "Sit down and catch your breath awhile. Clearly your mother's time has come but don't worry she is quite used to having babies by now. She will be fine. Let me get my bag and we can walk back to the mill together."

Despite his growing concern for his mother, Pierre was obliged to walk patiently beside the elderly lady as she gripped his arm tightly to maintain her balance on the muddy paths that led from the village downhill to the mill.

When they eventually arrived at her bedside, Pierre's dad had already placed a big kettle of water to boil on the fire in the chimney and had laid out a pile of clean cloth torn from old sheets that were beyond repair.

The old lady took one look at Pierre's mum and turned to Pierre and said "your dad and I can handle the birth, best that you go for a walk outside and only come back when you hear the new baby cry." Tom nodded at Pierre in agreement with the sage femme's words.

These seemingly innocent words, spoken calmly by the old lady, had the opposite effect to those she had intended. Rather than being naturally worried for his mum, poor Pierre was now petrified and he did what he always did when he was really worried, he came to find me.

He walked down the steep, slippery but by now well-trodden path from the top of the gully down to the water's edge and then leapt from the tiny beach, across a few feet of shallow water and onto the smooth rock where he knew he would find me.

"*Bonjour mon Pierre*," I whispered gently as he sat near to me, "I can see that you are worried for your mum."

"Oh my Ondine", he replied in a trembling voice, "I am so afraid that she will die and the baby with her. She looked so weak and I know that my dad and the *sage femme* are worried. That is why they sent me out of the mill."

Tears began to trickle gently down his handsome face and catch in the fair down that I noticed had started to sprout on his cheeks. All I wanted to do was to hold him, to comfort him, to give him my love and to tell him that all would be OK. But I had a vivid premonition that it would not be.

After what must have been about two hours, Pierre's dad suddenly appeared at the top of the path and called softly "you need to come home now, *mon chéri.*"

I could feel, and Pierre could hear, the sadness in Tom's words. We both knew the worst before anymore words were spoken. Pierre's mum had simply been too weak to survive the birth but miraculously she had managed to find some final strength to push out a tiny little girl who now greeted Pierre's return to the mill with a weak cry of anguish. The midwife was just completing her task of cleaning the new-born before taking her leave to go back to the village to find a wet nurse for the tiny mite. The new arrival in Pierre's family has been named Jessica. I often hear her crying, or I should rather say mewing, just like a little cat, as I pass by the mill.

Tom is now faced with a real dilemma: how to continue working, with Pierre's growing help of course, while looking after the new baby, Jessica, and the middle child, Patrick, an equally handsome but miniature version of Pierre.

Tom's problems appeared to have been solved by the arrival of the wet nurse. She came to the mill, a few hours after the passing of Pierre's mum, accompanied by a skinny little blond girl with plaited ponytails; her ten-year old daughter, Paulette.

Pierre later told me that Madame Tournier, for that was the wet nurse's name, had just a day or two earlier given birth to a little boy that had not survived more than a few hours. Thus her large breasts were painfully full of milk and she was desperate for a baby to help relieve her of her copious bounty.

I also learnt that there was a lot of gossip doing the rounds in the village about Mme Tournier for there was no Monsieur Tournier and, apparently, there never had been. Until now, she had been obliged to work as a housemaid and 'companion' while staying wherever she could. That seemed frequently to include in the homes

– and beds – of any of the village bachelors who had taken a fancy to her generous shape and large posterior. A real village scandal surrounded that poor woman!

But as Pierre had told me, "her problem is our solution. Not only can she feed Jessica and look after Patrick but she is willing to move into the mill and look after the home and even help my dad and me with some of the lighter tasks in the mill. I hate sweeping the floors and bagging the ground flour but she says that she is happy do that and her skinny daughter, Paulette, can lend a hand too".

The beauty of that solution was that Pierre had some extra free time and, for a few weeks, I begun to see rather more of him than I had previously.

The birth of Jessica coincided with some strange changes going on in the Sierroz. Downstream, I had heard that the water was getting deeper and little whirlpools had started to appear where previously the clear mountain water simply kissed the fine gravel that lined our river on its way to the Lake. I did not know what had caused these changes and so, intrigued, I journeyed far downstream to see what was going on.

In horror, I found that a group of men had blocked the water flow with a dam made of thick planks of wood held in place by large iron bars. The dam was causing the water to back up and now our once crystal clear water was looking cloudy and very deep, especially immediately behind the blockage. The poor trout and grayling that were used to living in the pristine waters of our river were obliged to navigate the sediment and mud in semi-blindness. My first reaction was to think that if only we could move the iron bars, the wooden dam would crumble under the weight of water and we would return the Sierroz to its former freedom.

But sadly that would no longer be possible for other men were working with machines, ropes and hoists downstream of the dam. I could see very clearly that they were building a sturdier, more powerful, higher and permanent structure of stones and cement, strengthened by yet more iron bars. The men were building this monstrosity to nature with a distinct curve that I heard them saying would provide even greater resistance against the might of the Sierroz. The only positive that I could see was that they had left a sort of gateway at the base – I heard the word 'sluice' being used by the men – where a mere trickle of water was able to emerge and proceed (flow would be a misnomer) down towards the lake.

In sadness, I went back to my higher and still unchanged part of the Sierroz and waited for further news. Two weeks later, I heard that the men had finished their work and the 'barrage' was now the height of three men while the water behind the barrage was rapidly getting forever deeper.

Pierre was then sixteen and working with his dad each day. Moving the numerous sacks of grain and flour had provided him with muscular arms and widening shoulders while his voice no longer croaked for he had developed a rich tenor's voice that he often used to sing local love songs to me. I loved him so much.

He told me that one of the reasons for building the barrage was to be able to make the river navigable from quite far upstream down to the dam. A small steamboat had arrived and the boat's owner was looking for a couple of strong young men to help with loading and unloading of people and supplies on to the vessel as well as shovelling coal into the boat's furnace. The owner had disingenuously named his boat 'Le Christophe Collomb'; no less. Of course this was partly in reverence to the famous explorer but mostly because the owner happened to be called Collomb! Monsieur Collomb was, like Tom, a miller but rather more successful and his family far, far richer.

Tom had given Pierre permission to work on the boat each morning because Patrick was then strong enough to help in the mill during Pierre's absence while a friend of Pierre's was willing to work the afternoon shift.

And the steamboat proved to be a relative success as the rich and sometimes famous came to the Sierroz from the nearby bath town of Aix-les-Bains to enjoy an afternoon of sightseeing and relaxation. Their trip involved chugging up the gorge and hearing about the geology and how the gorge had been formed over the millennia. The boat-owner (the aforementioned Monsieur Collomb) started off as the narrator but soon realised that Pierre had a voice and an appearance that appealed to the tourists, especially those of the younger and fairer sex, and so he was soon promoted to the position of Principle Tour Guide!

At the end of his third day as the principle guide, Pierre came to find me and immediately burst out laughing as he tried to tell me of the events of his day. As he calmed down from his fits of laughter I slowly began to understand what had happened. It seems that *le vieux* René, a lovable rascal and a well-known smuggler who frequently led his old donkey along the footpaths that follow the Sierroz as he made his way from Switzerland to Aix-les-Bains with his contraband, had been challenged by a team of three customs officers. He had been trapped by two officers appearing from one side of the trail and the third who appeared in front of him. He was far too old to attempt to run away back up the hill and could only see several years in prison awaiting him; unless … He surprised the customs officers, who imagined that they had made an easy arrest, by simply jumping off of the high bank of the river and plunging down into the Sierroz. Now, prior to the building of the barrage, *le vieux* René would simply have crashed into the jagged rocks fifteen metres or so down but, on this occasion, he jumped feet first into the deep pool that had formed beneath. Rather than coming back up to the surface where he would have been easily spotted by the officers, he simply swum underwater as far downstream as his retained breath would allow, finally resurfacing beyond the field of view of the customs officers but within sight of Pierre's steamboat, moored at the side of the gorge. *Le vieux* René waved at Pierre, as he worked on the boat, and swam behind the bow.

"Don't tell the customs men that you have seen me, young man!" beseeched *le vieux* René. To which young Pierre assured him that he would say nothing.

Back on the heights above the river, the senior customs officer asked his men "Which of you two will follow after him into the water?"

"Nah," they replied in unison, "he will already be dead after that steep fall. You know that the river is full of rocks and the current is vicious. That old man will not have survived the fall and we are not paid enough to get ourselves killed too. Anyway, we have the donkey and the contraband, that's good enough for today."

On the mention of the contraband, the officers turned around to where the donkey had been standing, but while they had been occupied by *le vieux* René jumping into the water, the donkey had simply wandered off. Try as they might to catch up with it, and they tried going in all directions, they failed to find him again. Rather embarrassed, they agreed that it would be better not to speak of the incident when they got back to the Customs Offices; *Le vieux* René was off scot-free!

Time passed, summer turned to autumn and then to winter and, before we knew it, buds were again bursting, birds were singing, the trout were migrating upstream to spawn – but far fewer since the barrage had been constructed – and everyone's thoughts turned to love; mine and Pierre's included.

Sadly, the object of Pierre's love – perhaps I would be more correct to say infatuation, surely not love – was sadly not me but rather a Parisian brat (my term) called Jeanette that Pierre first met on the boat in early summer and who then came back every morning to redo the tour. After about a week, it seemed that Pierre finally got the message that she was really interested in him and not the geology of the gorge or the trees that appeared to grow out of the sheer rock face.

Jeanette was fifteen going on sixteen and, I have to admit, that she was blossoming into a very beautiful young woman. Her heart-shaped face was surrounded by a halo of blond hair, often tied back with a pink ribbon. The obvious signs of her growing maturity were evident to me and rather too evident to my poor Pierre. He brought her regularly to our flat stone on the bank of the Sierroz where they sat closely together, occasionally chatting with me. But I could see that Pierre had difficulty keeping his eyes off Jeanette's pretty face and swelling bosom and, when they climbed back up the steep slope to the footpath that led back to the mill, poor Pierre could not help himself but stand back, admire and stare longingly at her rounding bottom as she progressed with difficulty up the winding path back to the top.

I whispered so often after him "oh Pierre, you foolish boy, can you not see that she is tempting you to fall in love with her and, once you have, she will leave you in sadness to return to Paris and go back to her ladies' school there? Be warned my love, be warned. She will break your heart."

I was sure that he would soon come to his senses. After all, I was here waiting patiently for him, and my love was so obvious.

But I was beginning to get worried that my prediction was set to fail because as the summer started to merge into early autumn and the heat of August, so evident in our region, began to wane, Pierre and Jeanette were still together and came almost every afternoon to sit on the smooth rock in the shade of the overhanging hazel nut tree and dangle their feet in the fast flowing water that rushed down from the millrace.

I noticed, with a little sadness and growing malice towards Jeanette, that they now chose to sit a little away from me, holding hands and often giggling when one or the other said something, even something rather foolish. The only thing that stopped me becoming really depressed was when they brought little Jessica to visit. On those occasions Pierre seemed to try to behave a little more sensibly in front of his five-year-old sister while Jeanette would lie back on the smooth rock soaking in the sun, and turning as brown as the ripening hazel nuts on our overhanging tree. Or alternatively, she would write on bundles of postcards that she told Pierre were for her friends and family back in Paris.

Little Jessica preferred to splash in the shallow and safe waters that lay between the bank and our flat rock. She adored having most of Pierre's attention provided her and happily squealed with pleasure when Pierre splashed her with the cool Sierroz water or built little gravel piles for her to knock down as soon as they were built. But Jessica's visits were too rare and, even when she did visit, her attention span was exceedingly short so that after only about half an hour, she invariably begged Pierre to take her back home to Mme Tournier, who she had started to refer to as *maman*.

The day that Pierre had been dreading for so long finally arrived in mid-September. His dearest Jeanette left for Paris in the morning leaving Pierre inconsolable; even by me. I had listened to them on the afternoon before Jeanette had boarded the steam train back to

Paris making all sorts of promises to each other. You know the sort of things that young lovers promise: 'I will soon return', 'I can never love anyone else but you', 'you must take good care of my heart' and more and more of that gooey stuff that young sweethearts spout at the end of holiday romances.

Frankly I could not wait to see the back of that young miss.

We say that where there is a yin, there is sure to be a yang but as events unfolded from my pleasure in seeing the back of that young lady – despite the obvious heartache for my poor Pierre – it would appear that my yin (to see the back of Jeanette) was to be repaid with an even greater yin a few days later. Here's what happened:

We had had several days of intense rainfall and the Sierroz was carrying much more water than usual and that water was particularly muddy and full of branches and broken pieces of wood. I imagine that the intense rain that had swollen our river to such an extent must have uprooted several trees further upstream. But I really did not know precisely why the river was in such a dirty and angry state. No matter.

At a break in the rain, I heard a series of happy squeals from Jessica which could only have meant that Pierre was playing with her; probably hide and seek or chase. A few moments later, I realised that it was a combination of the two because I could see Jessica racing along the upper path while Pierre was calling after her, suddenly in a rising and ever more panicky voice, "stop, stop Jessica. Stop. Do not go near the river."

But we all know how children are when excited. Hearing Pierre's raised voice only made Jessica more disobedient, she ran faster and then came charging down the steep and very slippery path towards me with Pierre hot on her heels. As she arrived at the bottom of the path, Pierre made a grab to grasp her arm but he missed and, laughing, Jessica leapt across the little stretch of calm waters and on to our flat rock. Sadly, for her, the rock was soaked after the several days of rain and she slid across it and toppled into the raging Sierroz, being quickly washed downstream.

Pierre did not hesitate, of course he did not. He dove straight into the river without a second thought ... and straight into my awaiting arms and my lover's embrace.

We are together until this day in the beautiful but ever changing waters of the Sierroz.

On hearing my story, people often ask what happened to little Jessica. Well, there was perhaps a certain amount of yang involved because she actually managed to grab hold of one of the myriad pieces of floating wood that were making their way down the river while the current – with no little help from me – brought her eventually to the right-hand bank where she was able to emerge cold, wet and dirty but safe from the Sierroz.

Other people try to blame me for the drowning of the Baroness Adele de Broc but, if you will excuse the pun, this was not caused by a little Sprite but rather by too much of the contents of a magnum of champagne. Blame where blame is due; it's only fair.

4

The Village of Pluvis

Very early in the morning, even before the village cockerels had begun to stir in their roosts, a tall slim figure began his descent through the pine forested slopes of le Revard, direction Aix-les-Bains and the Lac du Bourget. He was dressed all in black with leggings of a fur-like appearance, probably moleskin, a thick overcoat that dropped to below his knees and rose to a hood that covered his head and most of his face. It was bitterly cold in the high mountains and he was dressed accordingly. His footsteps left witness to his passage in the deep grooves he scored in the early winter snow. Where he came from and what was his ultimate destination, no-one knew but he.

After a hard thirty-minute trek, on a steep and continuous downwards trajectory under the towering pine trees and through the clinging brambles, he finally emerged from the thick forest on to a narrow trail frequented mostly by wild boar and muntjac deer. Travellers were rare in these parts since the forests were dense and packs of wolves roamed abroad. However, what kept most away from this region were the rumours that abounded about other elements, not of this world, that inhabited the forests and preyed on any foolhardy traveller. Thus few people would risk the mountain trails without adequate company, sharp weapons to ward off the forests beasts, and prominently displayed holy crosses of wood or iron or silver to protect them against the devilish entities. But this traveller seemed unconcerned by the dangers posed within the forest neither from its animal nor its demonic populations. He followed briskly the forest trail until it became broader and more trodden; signalling the approach to a human settlement.

The wider trail eventually led to a small hamlet of seven or eight stone and wood-built houses and his arrival was announced by the sharp bark of a scrawny dog tied to its home, an old barrel lying on its side. One look from the stranger was enough to make the dog whine, then fall silent and retreat into the relative safety of its kennel.

An equally early riser, a peasant farmer, was rinsing his face in the iced water of a cattle trough that stood outside of his home as the stranger passed by. The farmer called out a greeting of 'good morning', and was about to offer the stranger a hot drink to help him on his way, that was until the stranger glanced into his face from beneath his black cowl to provide his own friendly response to the greeting. The unspoken words of invitation choked in the villager's throat, he crossed himself rapidly and disappeared back into his home, bolting the door behind him. Such was the reaction that our traveller occasionally experienced during his journeys. Were such people fearful of his gaunt, pale features, did they sense a certain malevolence emanating from him or were they simply afraid of their own shadows?

The early morning sun began to appear as the traveller turned right on to the cart track that led towards the hamlet of Méry. He had decided to avoid the larger conurbations that surrounded Aix-les-Bains as well as the town itself with its myriad of coaches and diligences driven for the rich residents of this renowned spar town.

Two kilometres along the road leading to Méry, a cart laden with hay and drawn by a tired-looking white gelding pulled to a halt and the driver indicated with a gesture of his thumb that the traveller could climb into the back of the cart. The driver called back to the traveller that he was taking the hay to the hamlet of Charpignat and so he would be travelling through the fishing village of Le Bouget-du-Lac and continuing a few kilometres up the steep trail that ultimately led to the pathway across the Col du Chat. The traveller was told that he could descend the cart at any time as far as the turn off for Charpignat, he needed only to call out. This kind gesture was to take over ten kilometres or almost three hours of walking off of his journey. What good luck and what a relief for him to take the weight of his feet and close his eyes for a long nap.

As midday approached, the white gelding pulled to a halt and the driver called out a good day greeting to the traveller. His kindly greeting was echoed by the traveller's thanks as he descended from the hay cart on to the rough road that led up the steep hill towards the Dent du Chat. The cart continued on its way to Charpignat where the driver pulled into his barn to unload the hay. As he removed his pitchfork from the hay pile, he was surprised to find a small pouch attached to the handle; and even more surprised to find two brass pieces bearing the head of a now deceased ruler of the Duchy of Savoie.

Meanwhile, the traveller, now feeling refreshed after his sleep in the cart, strode out along the road keeping the bare rock face of the Dent du Chat in his forward vision. He followed the track ever upwards until, halfway to the bare rock, the trail reached a fork. The traveller took the left-hand trail knowing that it would lead him towards the Col du Chat, from where he could follow the narrow donkey track over the mountain ridge and then begin his descent towards the small but growing town of Yenne.

By mid-afternoon, he passed through the little hamlet of Saint-Jean-de-Chevelu and, less than an hour later, arrived at the picturesque town of Yenne. Initially, he had thought to seek shelter for the night in Yenne but, given the time he had saved by taking the lift in the hay cart and the fact that the weather had remained fairly clement since midday, the traveller decided that, rather than break his journey for the night in Yenne, he would continue westwards following the River Rhône's meandering path. As he walked into the late afternoon sun that was trying its best to poke through the gathering cumulus clouds, he marvelled at the force of nature that had carved the narrow track through the limestone rocks; probably created by a long forgotten mountain torrent. Without that narrow path, the impenetrable rocky barrier would have forced him to take a very long detour across the mountains or splash through the shallows of the river; neither alternatives that held any joy for him.

However, a little more than a kilometre after leaving Yenne, the traveller began to regret his decision not to stop for the night in the town as a heavy mix of rain and snow began to fall creating, in only a few moments, near blizzard-like conditions. He continued to trudge along the trail, evermore regretting his decision to pass through Yenne when, in the gathering gloom, just off to the right of the trail, he espied a humble abode of a single storey built of roughly hewn limestone. The smoke rising from the chimney promised some warmth for the tired wanderer.

He walked up to the house, marvelling at the way it sat perched on the very edge of a sheer cliff, appearing precariously balanced above the swift waters of the river some twenty metres below. The traveller called a greeting in the native Savoyard patois of the region and received in reply a shouted "come in and get yourself into the warm."

The occupant of the house proved to be a wizened figure of a man. Not a dwarf but rather a very short, stout and elderly person with a back so worn by past labours that he was almost bent double at the waist as he moved around the single room that served as kitchen, sitting room and bedroom.

"Sit by the fire, my friend. You must be frozen, please no shyness, sit, sit while I add more wood to the blaze."

As the traveller moved to sit on the single stool that stood close to the open fire, he saw a pot hanging from a hook attached to a long iron chain that came from inside the chimney breast. He could hear the contents bubbling inside while a most delicious aroma filled the air. A leek soup if the traveller's nose did not deceive him.

After twenty minutes of polite conversation, the traveller begun to feel warmer and removed his travel cape. He then accepted a bowl of the most delicious leek soup he had ever tasted and a slightly stale hunk of local bread that he broke up into the soup. When both had finished their potage, his wizened host dug back into the pot with a ladle and came out with two eggs, still in their shells, and placed one on the tin plate of the traveller and kept one for himself. After almost twenty-four hours of fasting, the traveller had to admit that his hardboiled egg was just perfect, and he said as much to his host.

"We are in luck today my friend because my two hens gave me two eggs. If one had let me down this morning, you might have had to watch me enjoy the egg alone." And he laughed out loud at the teasing good humour of his statement.

As was the norm in those parts, once the sun had dipped under the horizon and its afterglow had disappeared from the western skies, the wizened man excused himself to his cot across the room and removed one thin cover from his unmade bed. This he handed to the stranger and invited him to make himself comfortable on the floor close to the fire. Both slept quite soundly, awaking with the song of the cockerel that shared the chicken's enclosure with the two hens.

The traveller rapidly got ready to take his leave, thanking the old man for his hospitality and good company. He proffered two silver coins – a relative fortune for such a humble gentleman – as payment for the accommodation and evening fare but the old man would have none of it, stating that no payment was necessary. Instead he thanked the traveller for his excellent company and wished him *à Dieu*.

"I am sure that your hens will have laid you more eggs this morning, you should check" foretold the traveller as he walked out through the door and back on to the trail parallel to the Rhône.

"I can only hope my friend, I can only hope," the old man called after him with a chuckle.

When the traveller had disappeared from view around the next corner, the old man went to give a handful of grain to the chickens and check if, indeed, the hens had been kind enough to lay an egg, or perhaps two. He slid his hand under the first hen and, indeed, there was an egg awaiting him and, when he checked the second, there was another egg. As the old man drew out the second egg from under the hen he found, stuck to the shell by a small amount of dried excrement was a coin; a small gold coin. "Bless you my mysterious traveller friend" was all the old man could say as he wept tears of joy.

The traveller continued to follow the trail as it progressed towards the tiny hamlet of La Balme, that he saw was composed of only three small houses facing the river. He knew that here he would likely find the means to cross the Rhône in a small boat and leave the Duchy of Savoie behind him while entering into the realm of the French.

Twenty minutes after leaving his overnight abode, he arrived at the riverside, just as the sun began to make a weak appearance behind his back. With the extra luminosity, he immediately espied the small rowing boat used to ferry passengers across the river. It sat equidistant between the two banks but luckily the boat was moving towards him rather than going in the opposite direction. Nonetheless, while the distance to traverse was no more than eighty metres or so, he knew that he would have to be patient for at least another thirty minutes before the boat would arrive at its moorings. From his place on the riverbank he could clearly see the two oarsmen battling the fierce current that was forcing the boat further and further downstream. He knew from experience that the river would eventually allow them to land but probably several hundred metres away meaning that the oarsmen would then need to disembark and manually tow the boat upstream against the currents. Fortunately, large stretches of the riverbank on this side of the river, under instruction of the Duke, had been cleared of trees and the earth flattened to form a rough towpath or *chemin d'hallage*, as towpaths are called in these parts.

Finally, the traveller saw the ferrymen walking in tandem along the towpath on his side of the river with a thick rope over their shoulders pulling their boat behind them. Almost exactly thirty minutes after he had first espied them out on the river, they arrived back at the crossing point.

"Good morning to you sirs," the traveller addressed the ferrymen, "when you are refreshed, I would appreciate passage across the river."

"Our pleasure, friend, that will be two brass pieces for the crossing if you please" replied the stouter of the two oarsmen accepting the proffered coins. "Make yourself comfortable in the prow of the boat, we will disembark in five minutes once we have drunk a little ale to get back our strength after the last crossing."

True to his word after a quick swig from his flask of ale, the stouter man took his place on the left side of the central bench, holding his oar ready, just above the waterline. His fitter colleague, actually his younger brother, pushed the boat slightly out from the bank and, in the same well practiced movement, hopped over the bow and into the boat. He took his place next to his partner, picked up his oar and, in perfect precision, they began to row across the river using the Rhône's strong current to propel them downstream and westwards towards the beckoning French bank.

The traveller saw, with rather guilty pleasure, that the heavy late autumn rains had swollen the river quite considerably thus increasing the strength of its currents. He realised that this would mean that the boat would make landfall much further downstream than usual, taking perhaps a good kilometre off the distance he would need to walk today. But he also realised that the poor ferrymen would be condemned to haul their boat a substantial additional distance on the towpath to get back to the crossing point where two further passengers now patiently awaited their crossing.

As the river was slowly traversed, the ferrymen used their oars to guide the boat gently towards the far bank rather than trying to row into the fierce current. They made small talk with the traveller as they went and he replied in kind. At this time in history, detailed information on reasons for a trip, ultimate destinations and other such formal or personal specifics were never shared with strangers. Too many times in the past, a gullible traveller had said just a little too much to a road companion or in an ale house and found himself robbed or, worse still, with a slit throat.

After forty minutes or so, the ferrymen were able to bring their boat into the far bank and allow their passenger to disembark in

France. The traveller saw that he was very close to the almost ninety-degree bend in the river that signalled the position of the cart track that led off from the road for Brens and onwards to Belley, to the lovely little hamlet of Champtel.

The traveller thanked the two ferrymen for their kindness and effort, wished them a good day and set off at his usual rapid pace towards Champtel, soon disappearing from view behind the tall plants of balsam that dominated the river bank at this point and painted the hedgerow in bright pink.

"An unusual fellow, that," said the stouter of the two ferrymen to his younger brother, "but at least he did not quibble about the price of the crossing, unlike the majority of our passengers. Here ..." and he put his hand in his pocket and brought out the two coins meaning to pass one on to his brother. "what on earth, *appels-moi un fils de pute!*" as, instead of two small brass coins, he found that he now had two silver coins in his hand.

The ferrymen made their way back up the river, whistling and singing as they went. The rope they held together over their shoulders, as they towed their boat back upstream, did not seem to bite so hard into their shoulders as it usually did and even the current seemed less harsh as they covered the more than nine hundred metres along the towpath that led back to the crossing point where their next passengers awaited.

Our traveller was not so fortunate for as he walked into and then through the hamlet of Champtel, he felt the first spatters of rain and, by the time he reached the so-called main road, the rain had changed to sleet that left ephemeral snowflakes briefly speckling on his coat.

He turned left on the main road, in reality just a double cart track, as it made its way south from the episcopalian town of Belley into the southern Bugey. The traveller knew that, should he be so inclined, he could follow this road and it would eventually lead him to the beautiful city of Lyon. But he did not plan to make such a trip today.

A little more than ninety minutes after leaving the ferry, he arrived at the small village of Peyrieu. He was soaked and the sleet had turned to snow and he felt chilled through to his bones. He took refuge in the village *lavoir* or washing house bereft, in this bitter cold mid-morning, of ladies who traditionally used the plentiful flowing water to wash their clothes and bedsheets. However, he noticed to one side of the large flat stone that served for washing and scrubbing clothes that someone had recently left a metal pail of ashes that anyone could help themselves to while cleaning their clothes; ashes serving at this time as nature's detergent.

The traveller thrust his hands into the pail to try to capture some of the remaining ambient heat; and withdrew them even more quickly as his careless fingers found several hot embers quite near to the surface. He careful extracted a few of the embers and laid them into an old bird's nest that a pair of black redstarts had thoughtfully built to raise their chicks earlier in the year. A few puffs of breath and the dry hay and straw began to smoke, then smoulder and finally burst into flame. He laid several small sticks across the straw and soon had a small but warming fire underway.

The result of his long walk yesterday, the relatively uncomfortable night's sleep on the floor and the damp and cold of today persuaded the traveller that now was the perfect moment to take a brief nap. Within five minutes he was fast asleep next to the little fire and it was three hours later that he again opened his eyes, realising that he had slept far too long and that the snow had continued to fall outside.

"Blast", he swore softly to himself both because he had overslept and because he would now need to continue his journey through a thickening blanket of snow. He realised that he would likely not arrive at his next stop until well after nightfall.

He adjusted his cape and set off down the road towards his next waypoint. This was to be the elongated and twinned villages of Murs-et-Géligneux that ran alongside, but at the base of, some steep limestone hills where quarrying activities were frequent. This section of his trip was only about six kilometres so, in normal circumstances, perhaps only a ninety-minute walk. However, having overslept in the middle of the day left him feeling more tired than if he had foregone his overlong siesta.

The layer of snow deepened with each step and his journey appeared to become longer and longer as he trudged along the road, ever heedful of any large and pointed stones now invisible under the deep covering of snow. He also anticipated potential issues at the entrance to the village's chateau – really a large fortified house – but as he passed by the gated entrance, the owner and his workers were absent; probably and sensibly sheltering from the intensifying snowstorm.

Once through the village, he continued trudging through the snow for another kilometre and then took the left-hand trail. He had decided to pass the night in the little hamlet of Pluvis that was still two kilometres in the distance and sheltered in the plain of La Bruyère and a small distance from the Mont de Cordon. This small mountain; really a hill, housed the impressive and equally terrifying Chateau de la Barre on its western flank. Stories told of the chateau's oubliette that was rumoured to contain many skeletons of petty criminals that had been imprisoned and then, ... well ..., forgotten inside its round, fortified walls.

Finally, at around seven o'clock when the sun had sunk into the plains of Isère across the other side of the Rhône, the traveller saw the outline of the small hamlet of Pluvis begin to make an appearance through the billowing snowflakes. As he approached more closely, he was relieved to see smoke from several chimneys, signalling the presence of their owners, and the twinkling of candles behind hand-laced curtains. He knocked at the first door and called out, as is custom in these parts, that he was a traveller, cold after his journey through the snow, looking for shelter and any food that could be spared and that he had generous coin to pay.

He saw the curtains twitch as curious occupants looked out and then he saw candles snuffed. The unspoken response from the first several houses was clear. He was most certainly not welcome. He tried knocking at a door further into the hamlet, and then the next, always with a similar response. Finally, he arrived at the last door, knocked hard and repeated his request, adding that he was a God-fearing soul and asking for the occupant's succour. The door opened as he had hoped but what he did not expect was that the peasant stood in front of him holding his hay rake with all four points menacingly directed at the traveller.

"Off with you, if you know what is good for you", the owner said in a loud voice. "We want none of your kind here, now be off". And the door was slammed shut to prevent any futile debate.

The traveller was in a bind and silently cursed the villagers for their uncharitable actions. He did not have the strength to start walking either to the hamlet of Cordon that stood on the far southern side of the Mont de Cordon or to go back on his tracks and head north to the villages of La Bruyère or Brégnier-Cordon. What to do now? Blast those foolish and uncharitable villagers who so coldly turned him away.

Just as he considered perhaps trying to force a stable door and join a cow or an old nag for the night, he saw in the distance and slightly raised above his position in the valley, a small glimmer of light. Could that be another peasant hut placed away from the unwelcoming hamlet? He walked towards the light having no path to follow since the snow had obliterated any indications of a trail but he noticed in the faint moonlight that while the tips of willow bushes and marsh grasses poked through the snow all around, there appeared to be a straight line where no such bushes and grasses grew. A hidden footpath, he surmised, and so he walked carefully through the snow, being drawn like a moth towards the flickering light in the distance. The hidden path turned uphill until, after a further three or four hundred paces, the traveller came to a flatter area that led around the hill and directly towards the light. As he approached the welcoming blaze he noticed that, rather curiously, it seemed to be burning in the mouth of a cave.

Wary of the reception he had received in the hamlet of Pluvis and so as not to frighten the occupants of the cave, he called out in his kindest voice that he was a traveller and looking for shelter and a place to pass the night out of the blizzard and the cold night air.

He was surprised and delighted to hear in response the soft voice of a woman telling him to enter and be welcome to her humble abode.

As the traveller passed the fire at the cave's entrance, he saw that the occupant, who had invited him in so kindly, was a very old woman with a face composed of wrinkles and lank grey hair that did not completely cover her pink scalp. The ravages of ringworm had left many areas of her head bereft of hair that would never be able to regrow.

The old lady rose from her seat placed as close to the fire as possible and again bid the traveller welcome to her home that she told him the villagers of Pluvis had named '*La Grotte de la Bonne Femme*' (or old woman's cave) out of their warped sense of sarcastic fun to the plight of an old lady forced to live in a damp cave.

"Please sir, take my place near the fire, sit on the stool, warm yourself and let us share some of my nettle soup that is cooking over the fire".

The traveller's heart was immediately warmed by the smile that the old lady gave him: joyful, loving, welcoming and most memorable for the blackness of the single tooth that she possessed at the front of her mouth. The warmth took a little longer to return to his body but eventually did, aided by the pungent taste of the hot nettle soup.

After finishing their frugal meal, the old lady moved a little further back in the cave – it was really more a depression in the rock face than a real cave – and bid the traveller stay near to the fire and then wished him goodnight.

His soft but continual snores told the old lady that the traveller had rapidly fallen asleep but she remained awake far into the night. She had sensed that the traveller had been tense and she guessed that his pride must have been hurt by the uncharitable attitude of the villagers; with whom she had as little interaction as possible. She had felt his rage, and she believed that was not in his nature for he seemed a placid and gentle soul. Eventually she drifted into a light sleep.

During the night, she thought she heard (or was it a dream?) a loud rumbling, like a thunderclap but one that went on for several minutes. She began to stir, turned over on to her right side and slipped back down into a now dreamless sleep.

The next morning, she awoke to find that the traveller had already arisen and was busily stirring the ashes of the fire to raise a few red embers. He then placed a handful of dried leaves of the box-tree on top of the embers and instantly the fire burst into flame with much crackling. Twigs and dried branches from the spruce trees that grew on the Mont de Cordon then followed and to these he added some thicker branches of ash and hornbeam. Within five minutes, the fire was burning brightly and the interior of the cave had already begun to warm up.

The old lady called out a 'good morning' and then rose easily from her rustic bed, noticing that this morning she had none of her normal arthritic pains. "That must be due to the welcome heat from that fire," she said to herself.

She pulled her cloak around her shoulders and crossed to join the traveller as he now looked down from the ridge outside of her cave. She could not believe her eyes. The entire village of Pluvis, all seven houses and their outbuildings, had disappeared from sight and been replaced by a sinuous band of clear blue water that continued both upstream in the direction of Murs-et-Géligneux and downstream where the River Rhône lay. Equally surprising, but clearly not the first thing that came to her mind, was that the snow of yesterday had melted and the sun was just breaking through on the eastern horizon.

"But where did all that water come from and where have the houses of the hamlet gone?" she asked of the traveller who simply replied with a shrug of his shoulders. She tried again "what has happened to all the villagers of Pluvis?" but still she received no answer to her question and, indeed, never did.

Seemingly unconcerned about the fate of the village, the traveller thanked the lady for her hospitality and kindness, handed her some small coins and was about to take his leave when he seemed to have another thought. He gently placed his hand on the shoulder of the old lady and gave her his blessings. He then took his leave.

Where he came from and what was his ultimate destination, no-one knew but he.

After his departure, the old lady realised that she should go down to the village and see if there was any way she could be of assistance;

perhaps there were survivors or animals to help. As she walked down the rather steep slope that took her from the side of the Mont de Cordon, where her home was located, and along the path that had once led to the village of *Pluvis*, she noticed that the waters that had been visible only an hour previously were now rapidly receding. And, by the time her path arrived at the water's edge, all that remained was a small lake standing precisely where the inhabitants of the hamlet had, only yesterday, refused common charity to the traveller.

She stopped at the very water's edge, marvelling at its crystal blueness and feeling thirsty for the first time this morning. She bent down towards the surface of the water and cupped her two hands. As her face went lower to drink from her makeshift cup, she espied a stranger ... looking back at her from the water.

"How can this be my reflection?" she asked herself. But there was no doubting her eyes for another miracle had occurred. Somehow she had become a young woman again and, from her reflection in the clear water, a very pretty and comely one at that. The wrinkles were gone and her scalp completely covered in soft and lovely auburn hair. "Bless you, traveller," she whispered to herself.

She spent the next hour walking carefully around the perimeter of the lake but found no survivors: human or livestock, nor even any flotsam. To her eyes, the village had simply disappeared from the face of the earth.

As midday arrived, she heard the hooves of horses approaching from the direction of Cordon and, on turning to face them, she espied six horsemen coming towards her. From afar she recognised the noble *Seigneur de Cordon*, accompanied by four men-at-arms. The sixth person in the group was a handsome young man of perhaps twenty years of age. And by his dress and bearing, she assumed that he must be the eldest son of the *seigneur*.

The two noblemen dismounted and asked the old lady (perhaps now we should start to call her the beautiful young lady) whether she could tell them what had happened to the hamlet. She simply shook her head and told them about the noise she had heard during the night and the scene she had witnessed first thing in the morning, and how the upstream and downstream waters had then quickly retracted until only the lake remained; with Pluvis drowned in its crystal depths.

The noblemen decided that there was little that they could do for the poor inhabitants of the village, who had all certainly perished, trapped behind their locked doors. The *seigneur* remounted his horse, calling to his young son to join him. But the young man's eyes had been turned by the beautiful young lady. He replied to his father that they could not leave a young woman on her own at the destroyed village but rather should invite her back to their chateau that stood on the hillside overlooking the village of Cordon.

That young man and the beautiful lady were destined to be married and would go on to form the noble line of '*de Cordon*' which exists to the present day.

Several hundred years later, *la Compagnie Nationale du Rhône* or CNR received approval from the national and regional governments to excavate canals across the major meanders of the Rhône and, at the points where the river water that passed through the canals fell back into the river, the company installed hydroelectric power plants. One of these canals was planned to pass from the Rhône, near to Murs-et-Géligneux, through the plain of La Bruyère, cutting straight through le Lac de Pluvis, and continuing in a straight line until it met the other side of the meander a few kilometres away from the neighbouring village of Glandieu.

In early 1983, before the bulldozers could begin their work of digging this section of the canal, engineers were obliged to drain the Lac de Pluvis. As the water level fell under the force of the engineers' massive pumps, so foundations of an old hamlet began to emerge from the muddy waters and sediments.

We know that the River Rhône has had a capricious history, frequently changing its course over the millions of years of its existence. In pre-glacial times the river was far larger than it is today, the existence of the Grotte de la Bonne Femme on the side of the Mont de Cordon was certainly formed by the eroding forces of a far deeper and more tempestuous River Rhône. On the walls of the river cliffs around the site of the village of Pluvis can be seen numerous rounded depressions that we call locally '*les marmites de bonnes femmes*' (or old ladies' cooking pots). They are in fact the scars left by boulders and pebbles that got trapped in depressions in the stone cliffs and were then turned millions of times by the river currents, slowly grinding the limestone to their current circular shape.

Furthermore, only a few hundred years ago, so in relatively recent times, earthquakes and tremors are thought to have moved the Rhone eastwards from its bed some fifteen kilometres north of Pluvis and left behind the marshy and forested area that we now know as Le Saugey.

Can the fate of Pluvis be explained through modern geological logic or was the ire of our traveller responsible for the destruction of the hamlet?

I suppose that we will never know but what do you think?

5

The Face in the Curtain

I thought that I was immune to Covid. For at least six months, I have mingled with friends and family at so many events where one or more of the participants has later declared a Covid infection. Despite that, I have managed to remain symptom-free. Was I immune, was I one of the lucky few who remained asymptomatic even when infected or was it simply the resistance accorded me by a combination of the two vaccines I had received: Astra-Zeneca and then the new-fangled one from Moderna? I also wondered whether my natural good health had kept the virus at bay.

But silly me!

For today I am lounging on my large and soft deep red sofa feeling incredibly sorry for myself. I am trying to watch the latest episodes of 'Outlander' on Netflix and have a tray sitting on our coffee table that holds a tube of Dolipram, a glass of fruit juice and a few grapes on one of those pretty Victorian plates that my wife likes to collect. My vaccines and natural good health have failed me. I am yet another victim (albeit mildly) of Covid. And, we can put the blame for my infection squarely on my dear wife.

I have just enjoyed a rather relaxed three weeks in our country house, just a twenty minute drive from Aix-les-Bains, while my nearest and very dearest has been squatting our apartment in that lovely little town. During those three weeks, she has been 'taking the waters' (as the posher of the Brits might say) or attending *'la cure'* as we, the French, call passing twenty-one days being alternately smothered in mud then sprayed clean with a high pressure hose. In the UK this has been considered mistreatment of their senior citizens for rather a long time now, resulting in most of their spar towns receiving little custom apart from injured footballers and racehorses (and not to forget elderly masochists). But this is most certainly not the case in France where the Wrinklies queue up for such abuse and the state actually pays for it; believing (I presume) that what does not kill you makes you stronger.

But no matter about all that, what is important is that my dear spouse went off for the three weeks of torture and returned alive from her daily mud and spray treatment. And, after being away for three weeks, she kindly brought me back a present: the wretched Covid. It seems that everyone in the Baths was succumbing and then generously sharing it with every newcomer to *La Cure*.

She returned on a Saturday, started sniffing and moaning on the Sunday and by Monday was running a fever and coughing and snuffling. A well organised friend in the village, passed me a testing kit and, of course, she was positive. Now, being the kindly soul I am, I fetched and carried for my lady during her three days of suffering and my recompense was to be gifted the wretched Covid.

So you find me laying on my sofa trying to watch Netflix as the TV rams due to the lack of bandwidth in our little village. As I'm lying here, sweating under the influence of the virus and the Dolipram, I glance up at the beautiful curtains that my wife made several years ago from some lovely silk material that she brought back from one of our many trips to Thailand. While the background material is a soft yellow, it is covered with an intricate design of orchids and other tropical flowers that she knows I, as the family botanist, adore.

As I look at the curtains (while Netflix rams yet again) I notice that the space between two of the floral designs seems to describe a face. I am sure that everyone has had these optical moments when they see features, for example, in the shape of knots in a panel of wood or in the curve of stones in a wall. Indeed, as I type, I remember that, as a child, my mum's toilet used to remind me of an elephant's head, trunk, eyes and all!

But the face I can see does not seem to want to disappear. Even if I change slightly the position of my head. I can still make out his face, for it is the face of a pretty young man with blue eyes, reddish cheeks and a mass of curly, almost angelic, light brown hair.

Netflix starts up again pulling my eyes back to the television. 'Sassenach', the pretty English lady who has managed to pass back in time to be with the handsome rogue (Jamie Stuart) is trying to pretend that she really does belong in the eighteenth century. The obligatory love scene then follows that the directors have thrown in to distract us from all the things twentieth century that are so apparent in the lady's speech, dress and confidence. That scene serves to pull my eyes back to the screen until our Wi-Fi service provider again reneges on its over-priced contract and the picture freezes and Netflix's little wheel begins to turn once more. This is not a very opportune time to freeze the image, for the prim English lady is currently involved in some domineering of Jamie (... but enough said).

Getting a little bored ogling Sassenach and her (admittedly pleasant) charms, I look towards the window where the weak afternoon sun is sliding behind the hill that sits across the river in *Le Dauphiné*. Then my eyes move inadvertently up to the curtains. The face is still there. A little spooky, I feel. At first I try to think logically and tell myself that the impression of a face is merely caused by a strange play of the setting sun on the curtain. Then I think that perhaps my fever is making me a little delirious and that my raised temperature might explain the image more realistically. But no, a quick beep from my ear-held thermometer tells me that my temperature is only 38.1 centigrade, and that is insufficient to bring on a bout of high temperature delirium.

I decide to make a quick trip to the downstairs bathroom to allow Sassenach to get dressed in some privacy while Jamie goes off to try to convince the tribal chiefs that the Englishwomen, he has just bedded, is not a spy sent by the horrific English Lords that are currently trampling over the poor, kilted Scots.

While standing in front of the toilet bowl, I look up at the wood surroundings that enclose the back of our stairs that lead up to the first floor. There he is again: the same angelic mob of hair, the blue eyes and the red cheeks. I can make out his lips too. And, I know, it is only in my mind, they appear to be moving. Is he trying to say something too me? Lip-reading is not easy at the best of times but, in this case, are the lips forming English words or French ones or even patois? I simply cannot tell.

Bedtime arrives and after trying to read a few more pages of the adventures of John Rain in Paris with the delicious Delilah, an Israeli honey-trap spy, I put down my Kindle and turn off the bedside light. Sleep is a little hard to arrive seeing as I have moped about on the sofa all afternoon. But when sleep does finally come, it is light, intermittent and full of odd flashes of dreams and thoughts.

In at least one of the dreams I see the young fellow again. He is trying to speak to me and I am trying to respond but am finding listening to his words and providing answers extremely difficult; like trying to walk through deep mud – I cannot find the words to explain the equivalent – when trying to hear and speak in this dream.

My dream continues and I hear or rather receive a message, language does not seem relevant now, "see me!"

My dreaming mind seems to send back the message "I am seeing you, I have been seeing you all day. But why and what is your name?"

And back comes the response "no Pierre-Antoine, not 'see me', seek me, please, please, I implore you! I am Pascalino Cottalini from a small village near to Genoa. The French call me Pascal."

And now my dreaming mind understands the message. The young man called Pascalino or Pascal comes from Italy and is beseeching me to seek him out, to find him but where, where is he?

Finally, my befuddled brain and dreaming mind manage to send out the thought "show me!" And, in the dream, I am immediately transported to a dark room that feels cold and damp. The room has walls of exposed stones, a vaulted ceiling, a damp, pounded-earth floor and enclosed by a thick wooden door with large square-headed nails studding it at regular intervals. I cannot see any windows and the only light comes through a stone air-vent at the top of a wall, apart from the slightly open door that is. At the side of the room is a large stone basin with water dripping into it via an earthenware pipe that appears to be coming through the wall opposite the door. The half-filled basin is draining out through another clay pipe and this one disappears into the ground. I have no idea to where the water is draining. The room feels and looks like a cellar, indeed there is a metal bottle rack attached to a wall that contains some dust-covered bottles (I presume of local wine) and a couple of *dame Jeanne,* that likely contain *eau de vie*. I do not recognise this place although it feels somehow familiar. My house, for some odd reason, does have three cellars and I suppose that this room bears certain characteristics of each of them but again, it feels quite unfamiliar to me.

The final part of the dream that I remember on awaking with the crowing of my neighbour's cockerel is a scene, but not from this time. It is of a rural setting, indeed a setting that looks like it was filmed one hundred years ago in the courtyard of my very own house. I see a full hay wagon to which is tethered a brown nag. I see three people: the young Pascal, from my dreams, an older and bearded peasant with a clay pipe in the corner of his mouth, a cap sitting on his head and a pitchfork held in his left hand. The final character in the scene is a stout, middle-aged gentleman holding a stick; looking for all the world like a country squire from Gloucestershire.

A new day begins and, believe it or not, my Covid attack appears to have disappeared as rapidly as it arrived. Can the infection only last an afternoon? Believe me, it really can. I am now the living proof.

As is my habit – after all I am a career scientist and generally operate along a path of logic – I write down some rapid notes. I decide to start first with my dreams since we all know how hard it is to retain memories of dreams. Better I should scribble them down first before I begin to forget any of the details. Those notes are then followed by my memories of the events of yesterday afternoon.

When note taking is finished, I attempt to draw out the important details. It is clear that Pascal, the young man with the curly hair who begs me to find him, is the central character. The elderly peasant man near the hay wagon appears inoffensive but who really knows at this point? I make a note that he is likely to be a bit player, but perhaps also a witness to further events. The character of 'Farmer Giles', the squire, looks to be a bully, especially by his square shape and the manner he was holding his stick. But again, I decide to go carefully with trying to paint too many details into the scene I witnessed in my dreams. Nonetheless, he seems to be the boss around the farm and, I believe, not a man to be crossed.

The biggest question that my notes highlight is just where do I start and what am I even looking for? The young man hailed from Italy and so was likely a migrant worker. I decide to start on Google and find that Wikipedia has an article on Italian migration to France in which it is clear that many Italians became French following the annexation of regions such as Corsica and La Savoie. But my dream flashes seem to tell me that Pascal came to France later than that, indeed just prior to mass mechanisation of French farming. I am guessing – and this really is a guess – that the image I saw was from the approximate period of 1920 to (say) 1935. In other words, the inter-war years. Wikipedia tells me that there was a big influx of Italian migrants to France immediately after the end of the First World War when France cruelly lacked manpower due to the enormous loss of life she experienced in the trenches during the Great War.

So far so good, but all I have managed to do is to fix myself a very large canvas on which the finer details now need to be painted. How do I get to those finer details? I decide that rather than jumping into the deep end, so to speak, I will let my subconscious mind dwell on the issue while I set about doing something completely different and unconnected.

Since moving into my house several years ago, I have been promising myself that I will level the floor in my best wine cellar (remember I have three!). I need to make the floor level so that my metal wine racks stand more evenly and no longer risk crashing over when full of my expensive wine collection. Since each wine rack can hold fifty bottles and the average price of a reasonable bottle of Savoie or Bugey wine can range from seven to a dozen euros per bottle, the value of a full rack can easily run to five or six hundred euros; more if it contains champagne or good Burgundy.

The impetus to start the work in this particular wine cellar comes from the fact that it most closely resembles the one I saw in my dreams. The walls look similar and are built of the same stone, the ceiling is vaulted, the door is identical and studded with the same square-headed nails. There is so much similarity to the cellar I saw in my dreams but it is still not quite the same. There is no stone basin let alone the earthenware pipes and the room in my dreams appeared almost square while this cellar is elongated. However, the floor is the same being of beaten earth and very uneven: higher at the walls and lower in the middle.

I put a pickaxe, a heavy duty hoe, a shovel and a spade in my old wooden wheelbarrow and wheel it into the cellar. For no logical reasons, I decide to start on the left-hand side at the back of the cellar and run a drawstring from the far wall down to the front (or door) side. I allow a space of 40 centimetres from the wall and it is this area that I need to flatten so as to be able to arrange and then fix my wine racks to the left-side wall.

I begin trying to dig down into the floor with my spade but the soil is so compacted that I cannot make a dent in it. I then switch to the pickaxe and find that once the surface crust is pierced, the going gets considerably easier as I dig deeper. As the soil accumulates, I shovel it into the wheelbarrow. I manage to work down about a metre from the back wall when my hoe turns up a bone ... my goodness, don't tell me that I have found Pascal. The bone is a rib and when I place it against my chest, I find it fits relatively well to the size and shape of my own ribs. Of course, this is an exciting find and so I redouble my efforts but excavate with far more care. I continue to turn up more ribs, then parts of a shoulder blade followed by a humerus and what I believe to be a radius bone.

I decide to stop my digging at this point because, after all, I am at a possible crime scene. I go into the house, wash my hands carefully and then pick up the phone, thinking to call the local *gendarmerie*. As I check their number on Google, I have a flash thought: why not first get a doctor to have a look at the bones. After all, they could be the bones of a large dog or some other animal. Therefore, rather than calling the police station, I phone a friend who had been my GP for over thirty years until he retired recently. I ask him if I could bring some old bones over for him to check if they are possibly human. I get gently teased about my request but told to come over with the bones at lunchtime and eat with him.

We wait until after a very good lunch to inspect the bones and, it was not to be. He tells me that the bones are most certainly porcine and that we can even compare their shape and size with the bones that we left after eating some spare ribs at lunch! But more to the point, he shows me that the humerus I had found is considerably shorter than that of a human, and he is right, of course. In my excitement and anticipation of the find, I had forgotten to measure the humerus and radius against my own arm. I leave my friend, feeling a little embarrassed at my scientific error, but at least my wine cellar is not to be a crime scene just yet.

Driving back to the house, I cannot help but think of Pascal. I am more and more convinced that he came to France in the inter-war years and, even if he was around as late as 1935, that is still not far off ninety years ago. That thought brings to mind the 'Three Cavaliers' of my village, each at least an octogenarian and each a font of knowledge on village history. I wonder if they might be able to help.

I drive in turn to their three houses. The first call is on the village patriarch. His name is Louis and he is a sprightly 94-year-old. He was born in the village and has never left it but, nonetheless, he would only have been six years old in 1935. The next oldest is Henri at eighty-seven while the third, Georges, is the baby of the trio at *only* eighty-four. I invite all three to come around to my house the following afternoon to help me with some of my research and also to share a couple of bottles of the region's excellent white wine.

The next day, my friends arrive together in Georges' little 2CV, shake my hand warmly and take their places at the kitchen table. I first pop the cork off a chardonnay from Savoie and pour each a decent slug. I then start off by telling them that I am researching the history of my house and so would like their memories and also any stories or points of interest that they might have heard from their parents or even grandparents.

Henri starts off by telling me that a former owner was a cattle fattener who it appears bought small calves and fattened them up before sending them off to the market. This sounds interesting. Could this be stick-totting squire I saw in my dream? But this thought is quickly squashed when Georges chips in with the mention that it was sad that I did not get to speak to him before he passed away two years ago at the age of seventy-six. The dates for that gentleman simply do not add up to the fate of Pascal so I try to guide the discussion by asking if anyone remembers a room or a cellar in the house that had a big stone sink and perhaps running water that entered the sink via an earthenware pipe. Straight away Louis raises his hand off his glass and states that as a very young child he remembers splashing in the sink and that the room with the sink is underneath my house in the cellar. And indeed there is a cellar there but apart from the limestone walls, I can see little similarity to my dreams, especially since the ceiling of the cellar is not high enough to stand up in, plus the ceiling is not vaulted.

Louis continues with his memory and tells us all that the room should be on the right- or the East-side of the house. But I have to contradict him and say that there is no room in that part of the house, only on the West-side is there a cellar. Again, Louis insists that he may be ninety-four but he is not yet senile. The two octogenarians gently tease him, asking if he is sure and begging to disagree.

Louis stands up, grabs his walking stick and tells us that we should bloody well go and look then. So together we all go through the front door, past Georges' car, down the slope to the front of the house. I point out the door to the cellar, open it and duck almost double to get through the low doorway, then turn sharp left to enter the cellar. I remain with my head tucked into my shoulders to avoid banging my cranium on the low ceiling.

Louis looks inside and his face screws up in thought. We move back outside, putting our necks back into their right positions before he tells us that this is not the correct cellar. He knows that he is not wrong but is puzzled. After spending two long minutes in thought, he finally tells us that the house must have another room … over there, he indicates with his stick pointed at a blank wall of stone to the right of the cellar door. Inside the wall, I am sure that is where the sink was. It was in there, I know it. Someone must have built that wall, perhaps during some of the renovation work that was carried out after the second world war.

We troop back into the house and the Cavaliers ask me the obvious question of why I am interested in a hidden room with a sink when I am supposed to be researching the history of the house? My response that the sink is part of the history of the house is greeted with less than belief until Henri openly asks what is my real reason for all the questions about a room that does not appear to exist. The others join him in pushing me for a response.

I leave out all the real details of how I came to know about the Italian farmworker called Pascalino but say instead that I heard rumours in the village cafe about how an immigrant farm labourer who once worked in the village and stayed at my house came to disappear. First, Henri says that he has never heard such a rumour and then Louis and Georges mutter the same thing.

As if that last statement was a signal, each drains his glass and the three stand up and leave. As they troop out of the kitchen, each kisses me on the cheeks in a rather poor attempt to cover up their rapid departure and to show their continued affection for me. But I sense, rather I know, that they are hiding something from me and their collective embarrassment tells me that they know that I know. That was not the end to the session with three dear friends that I had anticipated.

The next morning, before I have time to finish my second cup of coffee, I hear a knock at the door and a familiar voice calling out to me. I shout a quick *'salut'*, leave the kitchen and walk into the sitting room just in time to meet Henri as he comes through the front door.

I have known Henri for almost forty years and it is he who convinced me to buy my current house and who then introduced me to the other cavaliers. Although a good twenty years older than me, we have always been close, more like father and son than simply friends. So I am relieved that he has come round to see me after yesterday's events.

He accepts a cup of coffee and sits down at the table with me. He tells me in an embarrassed voice that he is sorry how our session ended yesterday. How he worried so much afterwards that he had barely slept and that he had decided to come round and make a clean breast of events. He then starts to tell me about his family and, while doing so, he cannot stop a few tears running down his lined old face. He tells me that he and his sister and then his own three children, two girls and a boy, attended the local village primary school. All the children at the school were locals and most hailed from farming or wine growing families. As a young boy, slight in stature, Henri had suffered terribly from bullies who taunted him that his father had assassinated a migrant farmworker. Even when his own children went to that same school some thirty years later, they were still taunted by the rumours of what their grandfather was supposed to have done. Now his own children are well into their fifties, he had assumed that the rumours had died away and so was saddened yesterday when I mentioned that I had heard the story only recently in the local cafe.

He goes on to tell me about his father. He was a solid man and had a presence that could appear intimidating, even frightening, to people who did not know him but in reality he was gentle and would not hurt a fly.

I describe the stout man in my dreams who I had seen carrying the stick and then the older peasant holding the pitchfork. Henri quickly affirms that the first man is a pretty close description of his own father while the second man was not a peasant at all but the owner of this very house. Henri remembers that he passed away when he was about twelve years of age, so in about 1947 or 1948. He tells me that the man would have been pretty old when he died. Of course, Henri is curious about how I can describe them both so accurately.

I thought that this question might arise and so in advance had decided to be honest with him. During the next thirty minutes I tell Henri my story, leaving nothing out including the find of pig's bones buried in my wine cellar and the trip I had made to Dominque, my doctor friend.

When I finish my account, Henri tells me that his father knew of the rumours about having supposedly killed the migrant worker but he had always denied the fact, stating that one day he saw the young man at work in the neighbour's fields and the next he had disappeared. From that day on, no one ever saw or heard from Pascal again. The sudden disappearance led to rumours that he had been killed by Henri's father and those rumours have refused to die down, even almost one hundred years later.

Well, my canvas is beginning to fill up nicely. I now know who the three principle players are and I know that the scene was acted out here at my home. What I do not know is precisely where the missing cellar is located and whether the cellar has anything to do with the missing Pascalino. However, yesterday, Louis gave me a fairly clear idea where the cellar should be located, and I state that to Henri. He wants to know what I propose to do and, believing that actions speak louder than words, I tell him to come outside with me.

I go to my workshop and pick up a sledgehammer, a crowbar and a large torch. We walk to the front of the house and I take a mighty swing at the wall about two metres to the right of the door to the low cellar. Nothing happens after the first swing, nor after the second or third but when I hit the wall with the fourth swing, a large stone splinters apart and I can lever it out of the wall with the crowbar. Henri rushes forward with the torch and excitedly tells me to look. There in the beam of the soft torchlight sits the stone basin.

My manic moment with the sledgehammer now over, I hit carefully at the stones next to the hole and slowly but surely begin to make an entry for us. Once we have a space large enough to fit our heads through, I begin to remove the stones directly underneath my initial hole, forming a triangular shape. After all, we do not want the entire wall falling on our heads! Forty minutes later we are able to enter the hidden cellar, perhaps being the first humans to do so for almost ninety years.

I run back to my workshop and fish out an extension lead and two extension lamps. If we are to investigate the cellar, we will need to have a lot more light than a single torch can provide. Back in the hidden cellar, I am amazed at how accurate my dream had been.

Everything is exactly as I had dreamt except that the air vent and door are not there and must have been removed in order to build the wall that had hidden this spot for so long. The stone sink is there, the earthenware pipe coming out of the back wall is still there, and it is even still dripping water into the sink.

There are only two incongruities from my dream: a pitchfork standing against the wall and a hump shape to the floor in the back corner of the cellar. We look at each other for we are both thinking the same thing: Pascalino.

I collect my pickaxe and shovel from my worksite of two days earlier and use the point of the former to break the soil carefully at the top of the hump. It moves easily, as if almost freshly dug, and so I get on my knees and use my hands to move soil away. Henri takes the shovel and moves the displaced soil further into the cellar, freeing up space for me. Only ten minutes after starting, I come across a partly rotten coat and, as I pull this lose from the ground, a small tobacco tin falls out. Without thinking, Henri scoops it up and places it into his own pocket.

After the coat is removed, we quickly come across the evidence that we knew would be there. First we see a shoulder blade sticking out of the soil, then several ribs. Time to stop our work and get in the authorities. This time we really do have a crime scene on our hands.

We move back into my house feeling at the same time sad for what we have discovered and euphoric that this long running saga should soon come to an end. Henri rings the local *gendarmerie* and asks to be put through to the officer-in-charge. As it happens, she is known to Henri having recently led an investigation into an attempted theft of some of his farm machinery. He quickly explains the circum-stances of our discovery, says that we have withdrawn from the cellar and will await the arrival of the gendarmes who in fact screech up in their car within fifteen minutes of our call.

The two officers stick their heads into the cellar, see the partial excavation still lit by my extension lamps and go no further. Instead they first string yellow and red tape across the front of the hole in the wall, then report back to the *gendarmerie*. Their instructions are to stay put until the forensics team arrives.

In all the excitement, we had quite lost track of the time. When I check my phone, I see it is already thirty minutes after twelve; lunchtime no less. Henri comes to the kitchen with me and we load trays with plates, cutlery, glasses and a bottle of cold wine from the fridge. We carry a garden table and four chairs to the front of the house and then set up four places to eat. I fetch my electric plancha while Henri cuts several tomatoes and a raw onion and mixes his own style of vinaigrette. Two minutes later we have sausages and cutlets grilling on the plancha and, soon after, all four of us are sitting at the table having lunch and chatting like old friends; except that the police officers are in uniform!

Lunch is just over and the dishes stacked into the dishwasher when the forensic team (of two persons) arrives in their forensics van. The older of the two introduces himself as Dr Billiemaz and his younger colleague is presented only as Maria, his assistant and photographer. We provide them with outline details of our 'unexpected' discovery before letting them get on with their work. The good doctor and his assistant go to the back of their van and put on the over-wear of their trade before disappearing through the gaping hole in the wall and back into the cellar. I notice that the two policeman stand a few metres back from the room entrance and appear to be concentrating hard on retaining their lunch. I stand immediately behind the gendarmes and note that neither they nor the forensic scientists seem to mind me watching from a safe distance as work progresses.

The doctor bends down to the skeleton of poor Pascal and lifts out a skull with his gloved hand. Even from the distance of several metres, I can make out a full set of top teeth and marvel at the spring of curls that still remain attached to a portion of the skull. All the while, Maria is clicking away with her camera.

As the doctor examines the skull in more detail, he turns the back of the skull to face us and declares the likely cause of death ... a neat hole drilled through the back of the head. He then points to the pitchfork, still standing against the wall where we had found it when we entered the cellar for the first time, and tells us that it certainly caused the hole. Maria is still flashing away with her camera taking photo after photo of the bones so far revealed, of the back of the skull with its neat, round hole and of the pitchfork standing against the wall.

The fact that the pitchfork is the likely death weapon makes me feel rather good for Henri (but not so good for the poor Pascal) because I suddenly see the proof of guilt move away from Henri's dad and over to the former owner of my house. Why else would Pascal have shown me in my dream that person holding the pitchfork? I have another thought; the now prime suspect was holding the pitchfork in his left hand. Could he be a leftie and, if so, will that fact be picked up in the autopsy thus adding weight to my suspicions? I keep that thought to myself believing that time will tell.

After working for around two hours in the cellar, continually taking photos as their work progresses, the forensic team finally bring in a stretcher with an open body bag and begin to load the body remains and clothes into the bag. The bag is zipped and placed into their van, still on the stretcher. The doctor takes the gendarmes to one side and has a quick conversation with them. They go into the cellar and bag up other items, including the pitchfork, and these are also labelled and then placed in the forensics van. The doctor and Maria drive off but not before promising to keep us informed of their results.

The two gendarmes then thank us for lunch and bid us goodbye, stressing that the cellar remains a crime scene and we should not cross the restricting tapes. They anticipate returning the following day with an officer to make final checks.

Henri and I go back into the house and I pull out my bottle of *Marc de Bugey* that I purchased *chez-Angelot* in Marignieu and pour each of us a good slug; after the adventures of today, we definitely need it. As Henri lifts his glass towards his mouth, his hand stops in mid-air and he swears softly. He puts his hand in his pocket and brings out the tobacco tin that he had picked up from the floor. Both he and I had imagined that the tin would contain nothing but tobacco but when Henri opens it, we find that instead it contains a very small notebook and a pencil stub.

Curiosity gets the better of us and we open the delicate little book to find pencil writing covering almost every page. The language used is Italian and neither of us is sufficiently fluent in that language – despite it being a Latin language like French – to be able to decipher too many words.

Henri suggests that we should drive up to the *gendarmerie* and hand the tin with its book over to the gendarmes. I have a slightly different opinion as I am too curious to let the book go away so rapidly. Instead, I suggest that we should translate sections and see what Pascal had written about. Henri's puzzled face reminds me that he will be ninety in a couple of years and perhaps does not know about the recent advances of translation software. I tell him, we can enter some of the phrases in the book to 'Google Translate' and see what Pascal had written.

The rest of the afternoon and much of the evening is spent with me typing in phrases and seeing what translations Google comes up with. At the same time as I work on the computer, Henri uses a magnifying glass to unravel the more difficult Italian words and jot them down on a sheet of paper for me to type into the computer. As we make slow but steady progress with the Italian to French translations, I copy and paste the resultant French text into a blank Word document.

By the time we both reluctantly agree that we are too tired to continue any further, I have twelve foolscap pages of text and there remain only a little more that a half-dozen pages of translation still to be completed. I walk Henri to his car and, as we say goodnight, I tell him to come around for breakfast tomorrow when we can finish the translation and then hand the tobacco tin over to the gendarmes. Before getting into bed, I print off the pages we have translated so far, and read Pascal's narrative.

On the first couple of pages, Pascal describes how he had lived in the little village of Aggio that lies about fifteen kilometres north of the port of Genoa and how he had decided to come to France in 1931 to find work during the Great Depression that had hit Italy especially hard. He was seventeen years old at the time and, by a series of coincidences, made his way to our village and found work for the farmer who had once lived in my house. The farmer allowed Pascal to sleep in the large barn that is attached to the side of our house while the farmer's wife ensured that Pascal was fed.

Pascal states that the farmer was an 'old man' but what a seventeen-year-old considers old, I can only guess but I think he was probably in his fifties at the time. In contrast, Pascal describes the farmer's wife as being 'kind on the eyes'; make of that what you will!

As I read on, there follows considerable detail about his work, about the weather and about the few local friends that Pascal has made. The topic changes when I get to the tenth page of his little notebook. Now I find that Pascal is attracted to the farmer's wife and he writes that the feelings are mutual. Soon I am reading of a crazy love affair between the young man and the married women. Pascal begins to write about plans they are making to go away together but he sensibly writes that he has told his new lover to be extra careful to hide her feelings away from the old man. She in turn has seen the practical side and tells Pascal that they would need a considerable amount of money before they could go away together. He writes in his notebook that she has a plan ... but for that I must wait until tomorrow when we will translate the last few pages.

Henri arrives at 8 am and, after giving him fresh coffee and a croissant smothered with my homemade strawberry jam, I pass over the twelve printed pages for him to read while I excuse myself to go off to my study and complete the final translation. He joins me fifteen minutes later and tells me that now we have motive – and that motive, thankfully, has nothing to do with his deceased father.

I flick through the remainder of Pascal's notebook and see that the last three pages are blank, so only four more to translate. The first page contains little more than a young man's eulogy to his love. The second tells of how the farmer's wife has discovered the farmer's stash of gold coins and has handed them over to Pascal to hide before they run off together. The final written page contains a little drawing, a simple map, with four words written, curiously in English: 'X marks the spot' (I presume he was afraid to write in French or Italian in case his notebook was found before he could retrieve the stolen treasure).

Pascal had attempted to draw that little map in three-dimensions and I can see that the place (room?) is four times as wide as it is long, just like my cellar where I was working only a couple of days ago and found the pig bones. Could it be? We will soon find out ...

I show the little map to Henri and together we load the wheelbarrow with pickaxe and shovel and go across to my wine cellar. According to the map, the X is in the left-hand corner as we enter through the cellar door. Henri tells me that everyone who buries valuables always buries them in the corner of a room; so that they will not forget the exact spot. The only problem, he goes on to tell me with a laugh, is that everyone else knows this habit too. So if you want to discover a rich man's stash, always dig holes in the corner of rooms!

It takes us just over five minutes to dig a hole about sixty centimetres deep before my shovel makes a clunk against something hard. A quick dig with my gloved hand and we have found another tobacco tin. This time containing a little bag made of dark material closed with a drawstring that proves to hold thirty-five gold coins. Louis d'Or, Henri tells me, and I know that they are now worth a total of close to €10,000 at today's gold price. Do we hand the coins over to the gendarmes or keep them? I then have another thought and explain to Henri, he nods his head in agreement. We carefully remove the little map from the notebook, it slips out easily and without tearing, and then put the book back into the first tobacco tin.

I make a quick trip to the *gendarmerie* and hand over the original tobacco tin to one of the gendarmes who had been at my house yesterday. I state how and when we had found it and apologise for forgetting to give it to them earlier but, I was sure they understood that emotions were rather high. I am told, no issue at all. And thanks for the tin and of course for lunch yesterday.

As I am about to leave the station, the forensic doctor appears from another office and calls to me to join him in the room. The gendarme follows me in and hands the tobacco tin over to the doctor and then leaves. I am offered a seat and the doctor explains that the initial examination of the bones show that the body is of a young male of approximately twenty-years-old, that he has been in the soil unmoved for at least eighty years. This means that the police will not be looking for a murderer. He goes on to tell me that the cause of death was clearly from the pitchfork that we found propped against the wall as the cranial entry hole matched precisely the left-hand fork. The presence of dried material and hair on the fork adds weight to his thesis and so it will be DNA-tested to confirm that it matches the body.

I then make a very elemental slip. I say that I feel terribly sad that poor Pascal was killed at such a young age. The doctor is smart and he immediately picks up on the fact that I seem to know the name of the victim. He quizzes me about how I know and my only response is to mention the long-held village rumour about the missing farmworker. But that is not enough explanation for him because while the rumour of the disappearance of a migrant worker is well known in the village, no-one could put a name to the young man. So, how could I?

Good point. I cannot really tell him about my dream and all the consequences of that dream for fear of being carted away in a straitjacket and thus I confess that I looked at the first page or two of the notebook inside the tin; sorry!

A quick smile from Dr Billiemaz and a single word: naughty.

Three weeks pass and I receive a call from the *gendarmerie* to tell me that the body has been officially identified as Pascalino Cottalini from a little village called Aggio near to Genoa in Italy (the gendarmes must have gone through at least some of his notebook). A middle-age lady has been traced to the village and has proven, by

DNA testing, to be a close relative; indeed, a grandniece of Pascalino. The remains are just being released to her and she has said that she plans to inter the young man in the family tomb at the cemetery in Aggio.

I ask if they know when the funeral will be as I would like to attend and pay my last respects. I am given the telephone number of the mayor's office in the little Italian village and told to speak with them. A quick call to Italy, thank goodness the mayor could speak some English and a little French, and I learn that the funeral is set for the day after tomorrow at eleven in the morning.

Henri and I pack small suitcases and the following day we set off to travel the four hundred kilometres or so that separates our little village in Savoie to Pascal's even smaller village near Genoa. Before departure, I log on to Booking.com and book us two rooms in a sea-front hotel in Genoa and, after almost seven hours on the road, we pull into the parking lot of our little hotel.

The following morning after breakfast, we go back to our rooms and get dressed for the funeral and slowly drive the fifteen or so kilometres up the incredibly windy mountain road to Pascal's tiny village. We hear the church before we see it as bells ring out for the return of their lost son. We have timed our drive perfectly because I see from the car clock that we have arrived twenty minutes before the service is due to start and there is still room to park at the church.

As we get out of the car a women dressed entirely in black with a scarf covering her head comes hurrying across to greet us with hugs and two cheek kisses each. She introduces herself as Elena Cottalini, the grandniece of Pascalino, and she said that she was hoping we could make it to the funeral after our recent call to her local mayor's office. While Henri plays the perfect gentleman, I cannot hold my emotions and feel copious tears well up in my eyes and begin to flow easily down my cheeks. You see, Elena is the perfect image, I mean a real colour photocopy of Pascalino from the blue eyes to the reddish cheeks and that mass of curly, almost angelic, light brown hair that refuses to remain contained by her black headscarf.

I excuse myself to Elena, telling her that I had a feeling of *déjà vu* as she is the image of her granduncle and that I am so happy that Henri and I have been able to play a small part in returning Pascalino to his family and to his home. Elena is either too overcome with emotion at seeing my tears or simply too polite to ask how I know what Pascalino looked like.

The little church is packed to the brim for the funeral service. Elena leads us to the very front pew and sits her eldest son, in his mid-twenties, between Henri and I. Once we and Pascalino's family are seated, the congregation come through the door and take their places. Finally, two pallbearers carry Pascalino's small coffin to the front of the church facing the altar.

All the ladies are dressed in black, the men wear their Sunday best while the children behave perfectly for most of the ceremony. The priest conducts the service in Italian but when he reaches the eulogy, Elena's son leans across at intervals to translate for us. The priest tells the audience of how Pascalino came to be reunited with his family and points out Henri and I as the two Frenchmen who had discovered where his body lay and how we had ensured that he was finally brought back home.

As the service ends, we walk out of the church directly behind Pascalino's coffin into the bright sunshine of an early October's day. But it was not just the sunshine that dazzles our eyes but dozens of camera flashes. It seems as though the entire Italian press corps is present, that is until I see TF1, EuroNews and BBC-labelled cameras zooming in on us, under the careful eye of three *carabinieri*. We speak quickly to Elena and then, with her agreement, ask her son to address the journalists. We jointly promise to hold a press conference providing that they allow us to complete the funeral of Pascalino in complete dignity. Only an American journalist from a well-known news channel tries to break the agreement but he is held back by a well-placed *carabinieri* elbow in the nether regions.

We walk behind the coffin into the grounds of the cemetery that adjoin the church and then watch as his body is finally laid to rest in the family tomb.

"Goodbye Pascal and thanks for the adventure," I gently whisper.

We hold the promised press conference and, because it is clear that Henri and I will have the most questions to answer, suggest that Elena should speak first on behalf of her family. Of course she never knew her granduncle but tells the stories about him that her own father and grandfather had told her.

The attention then switches to Henri and me. We have agreed to gloss over the events and simply say that we found his body during renovation work at my home and that the details of Pascalino's identity were, luckily, contained in his little notebook. This seems to pass muster with the journalists and we are able to join the funeral wake and chat to those members of the congregation that are able to speak in French with us. But we realise that we should not linger overlong. We should let the family and village friends take centre-stage and so begin to say our farewells.

We walk back to our car with Elena and her son, promising to stay in contact. We exchange the customary cheek kisses before Henri hands a little bag made of dark material closed with a drawstring and tells Elena that Pascalino would have wanted her to have it.

6

The Bat Cave

Charles lived in a small village in the ancient Duchy of Savoie. His village possessed – and actually still does – only two claims to fame: a magnificent waterfall (or *cascade* in Charles' native French) and the fact that one hundred years previously, some Jobsworthy (oh yes, they existed then too) decided, on a whim, to break the little village into two halves. He, M. Jobsworthy, used the beautiful waterfall and the stream that it feeds as a natural geographic boundary line to split the tiny village in two and then, as if to compound his foolishness, assigned each half of a perfectly normal rural village to different communities. Each community with its own elected mayor, village council and budget. Thus, from then on, there were twice the expenses for the local populations to support. A clear example (if yet another should be needed) of how civil servants love to spend other people's money.

At the time this story begins, Charles was 59 years old and worked for the local council (the one that controlled the half of the village that sat to the right of the cascade as one looks at it). He was competent enough in his job which involved keeping the commune clean, the hedges trimmed and flowers planted in spring. In addition, twice a year he visited every house in the commune (only the ones to the right of the cascade, of course) and recorded the readings of each water meter.

In common with the two other *cantonniers* or maintenance men in the right-hand commune, the surest place to find Charles and his colleagues, should you have need of their assistance during the working day, was not outside tending the flowerbeds but safely snuggled in the aptly named *Café de la Mairie*. This café sat, not surprisingly I suppose, right next door to the council offices of the *Mairie*. Mid-morning was always considered the opportune moment for our *cantonniers* to partake of '*un petit blanc*' or glass of white wine. In less than a couple of hours, just before their lunch hour (of course lasting for two; *mais bien-sûr deux heures, il ne faut pas exagérer non plus*) their preference for their aperitif invariably changed to a long, cold glass of milky-looking *anis*. While they ate their *déjeuner*, ravenous after a hard morning at work, their preference usually changed to something red and local while in the late afternoon they either switched back to *le petit blanc* to quench their raging thirsts or, when the weather was sufficiently warm, to *une petite pression de bière blonde* as their half-pint of draft lager is called. But the reader should not be overly concerned, for these were not three rampant cases of advanced alcoholism that I am describing here, shudder the thought. Rather our team of municipal workers considered that they were providing considerable support both to the national economy and to an important local enterprise aptly nicknamed *"Chez Fifine"* by the team of council workers in honour of the buxom barmaid who served their drinks and meals and often led in their lewd jokes.

While in work their daily adventures were highly similar, it was in how they made use of their freetime that the real divergence between the three arose. Henri, the oldest of the *cantonnier* at sixty-one, was an avid fisherman and spent days (and sometimes nights) trying to catch carp from the local gravel pit that fell within the boundary of their commune (the one to the right of the cascade, that is). His largest catch to date was well over twenty kilogrammes and he dreamt of soon crossing the thirty kilo mark. His two colleagues permanently teased him that the only way any fish in that lake would ever reach thirty kilogrammes was if he continually stuffed them full of the high protein boilies made from a mixture of fish meal, strawberries and garlic that he so favoured as bait. Apart from the strange composition of the boilies, the other peculiarity about Henri's fishing habits was that everything he caught, he immediately released alive back into the lake! Henri was a true 'No-Kill' fisherman and his friends had long since given up asking him 'why bother?'.

The other *cantonnier*, Gerard (called by everyone Gé-Gé) was slightly younger at 58 and an inveterate hunter, belonging to the hunting club of the commune (the one to the right of the cascade, that is). He spent every Sunday throughout the long hunting season sitting on a raised wooden seat, with his back to the local roads and awaiting wild boar (*sangliers*) or muntjac deer (*chevreuils*) to break cover from local woodlands or maize fields. His role was essential for he was the keeper of the hunt bugle and his role was to blow long blasts when he spotted a *sanglier* or a *chevreuil* breaking cover. The bugle blasts brought fellow hunters charging out of the forest or the maize fields and was followed, in only a few seconds, by a broadside of shots sounding for all the world like the outbreak of the next world war. If mother luck was smiling, one of those bullets might just hit its mark and not wing another hunter, as sometimes happened.

Having been a hunter for more than forty years, Gé-Gé held an incredible club record. No, not for the length of his membership, that indeed was one of the longest in club history, but for never having managed to hit anything other than a fellow hunter's dog (the reason he was now permanently banned to the spotter's seat). Gé-Gé was justly proud of his record for while he no longer bothered to load his rifle with the expensive cartridges or bullets that most of his fellow hunters used and wasted, he still received a decent portion of any small or large *gibiers* that the other hunters managed to kill. But the *real* reason that he attended the hunt meets were for the lunches that the club provided at midday. The club counted itself lucky for two reasons. The first was to have *M. le Maire* as a paid-up member and, for that privilege, he ensured that the hunt, rather I should say the hunt association, received a generous handout from the commune's kitty. And the second was that the club had, as an associate member, a retired ex-chef called by everybody '*Le Grand*'. *Le Grand*, as his nickname implied was huge (as in 130 kg huge) and he was also an excellent chef. Each week while the more active hunters tried to keep up with their pack of howling dogs and Gé-Gé sat on his high chair proudly holding the bugle ready to blow, *Le Grand* rustled up enormous pots of the most mouthwatering stews using meat from previous hunting successes and boxes of vegetables donated by members from their vegetable gardens.

The best part of the day, as far as Gé-Gé was concerned, was the copious amounts of free alcohol, paid for by the generous donations that *M. le Maire* approved each year, that were liberally poured into ever empty glasses before, during and after lunch. Really, Gé-Gé's only unexpressed regret was that the club refused vehemently to buy their local wine from the 'Chez-Jean Vineyard' since, shudder the thought, Jean was the president of the hunting club belonging to the commune placed to the left of the cascade!

But what of Charles? What were his pleasures outside of the work environment? After all, it is he, not Henri nor Gé-Gé, that is the prime character of our story. Well, if I were to ask my readers to guess what his hobby was, I am prepared to bet that no-one, but no-one could come up with the correct answer. Why? Because Charles, the humble *cantonnier* responsible for reading water meters in the right hand commune was, in fact, a well-respected speleologist; a cave explorer, no less.

Despite the significant costs involved, he spent frequent weekends travelling with other members of both the Aix-les-Bains and the Annecy speleological clubs exploring caves and grottos right across France and even into Eastern Europe.

On the occasion of his fifty-fifth birthday, he was honoured by the X-Times newspaper with a front page spread that was, in turn, picked up by several national titles plus a TV news channel. The X-Times story told how he had started his hobby as a young man and then, as his strength, skills and experience grew, he was progressively asked to lead larger teams in more difficult and dangerous surroundings. He also mentored several national and international, and quite renowned, cavers that went on to greater things. One of his former trainees was none other than a member of the team that rescued the twelve Thai schoolchildren belonging to a local football team that, in the company of their young coach had rather foolishly entered and then got stuck in a deep cave system in Northern Thailand.

Sadly, Charles' moment in the spotlight proved to be just that, a very brief moment. For, almost immediately after being hailed as a local hero by the newspapers, during a particularly difficult descent of a cave system in Romania, he ruptured the anterior cruciate ligament in his right knee. He was stretchered out of the cave, a six-hour adventure, and airlifted by Romanian military helicopter to a hospital in Bucharest where an immobilisation boot was applied to his leg. From there an air ambulance took him directly to the Chambery-Savoie-Mont-Blanc airport; thank goodness for the very expensive insurance cover that the international speleological team maintained.

But, despite the excellent minds and surgical hands of the team at Challes-les-Eaux, the damage was done and his more extreme cave exploration days were officially over. The rescinding of Charles' 'Advanced Potholing' licence by the national authorities was a bitter-sweet moment for him but one that he knew had to arrive eventually, just not yet. To be honest, he had been aware for a couple of years that his exploration days were counted, even before rupturing his ligament that is, for he suffered in silence from acute arthritis in his fingers and wrists. This silence enabled him to pass his annual medical for the renewal of the potholing licence but his painful affliction weighed heavily on his conscience for he knew he would soon become incapable of hoisting himself up ropes in some of the deeper caves he loved to explore. At such time, he realised, he would become a real danger not only to himself but also to his fellow speleological team mates. With the removal of his advanced licence, Charles was able to stop worrying about being a liability within the caving teams. However, this was replaced with a bigger dilemma of what to do now to occupy himself when not at work. The very thought of sitting on a highchair every Sunday during the hunting season with Gé-Gé or going carp fishing with Henri filled him with horror. He must find something else to interest him, but what?

His son and daughter, both schoolteachers, solved the issue for him; or rather Milka solved the issue for everyone. Milka, named after an advert for chocolate bars covered in purple cows, was a lovable puppy of rather *mixed* heritage that Charles' two children obtained from the Annecy-based Canine Rescue Association. The notes that accompanied Milka during her transfer to Charles' children told a sad tale, first of neglect and then of abject cruelty. It appears that she was discovered by a municipal worker at a recently abandoned gypsy encampment on the outskirts of Chambery. Milka along with six of her siblings had been placed inside a plastic dustbin bag and abandoned at the site when the travellers moved on to their next location. It was by pure chance that one of the municipal clean-up team saw, in her own words 'the sack twitching' that anyone bothered to look inside. Of the seven puppies, three were already dead and the other three succumbed within a few days despite the rescue association's best efforts to save them. Only Milka survived, a relative miracle according to the association's veterinary surgeon since, when discovered, she was of an age that she should still have been with her mother and suckling mother's milk. Milka had spent the next couple of months at the association, first being bottle-fed, then slowly introduced to finely minced semi-liquid foods and from there to more solid food. At an assumed age of sixteen weeks, the puppy had received three sets of vaccinations and was then considered old enough to leave for a caring family.

Milka could never win a beauty contest or even a character one but she had a certain *'je ne sais quoi'* about her that it was impossible to put a finger on. There was something cute, amusing and beguiling about her. What did not help was that her head always appeared too small for her body, her face and body were predominantly ginger; not brown or buff but ginger nor that her tail consisted of only six vertebrae when the average should be somewhere in the region of twenty. The Vet at the association confirmed that her tail had not been docked but rather was a genetic peculiarity that had appeared from her very mixed breeding!

As soon as Charles laid eyes on this tiny almost helpless bundle, he was smitten and Milka responded to Charles as though this was her long lost mother. To say that the pair became inseparable would be to downplay the word. Wherever Charles went, the young puppy followed. He could not even go to the toilet without Milka first scratching at the door and then starting to whine to be with him; just to lay across his feet as Charles contemplated the affairs of the world from the toilet bowl. At bedtime, Charles' long-suffering wife was obliged quickly to lay down the law: 'Milka get off of the eiderdown' but not before Charles had positioned the puppy's basket strategically close to the foot of their bed.

As Milka grew from a puppy to a young dog, she allowed Charles a little extra freedom in that she progressively accepted his absence for work during the day without whining overmuch. Nonetheless, her whines of sadness (or were they protests of displeasure?) were replaced by a moping, hangdog expression that told all around her that she was not amused, indeed that she was incredibly sad. A human psychiatrist would have diagnosed her behaviour as 'abandonment syndrome' if it had been witnessed in a child but for Charles wife, Milka was simply being a *prima donna*!

Milka's demeanour always changed as soon as Charles walked through the door at the end of the day. She turned round and round him like a whirling dervish with her tail (all six vertebrae of it) rocking backwards and forwards in pleasure. Time for Charles to take Milka's lead and go straight back out for a walk – sometimes he remembered to give his wife a quick peck of hello on the lips but more often than not he forgot.

Their walk always followed the same path: first, along the road from his house to the cascade where Milka invariably stooped on the scrawny patch of weeds to relieve her bladder. Next, she would eat mouthfuls of green grass (really!) leading Charles to wonder if she was not at least part-goat. After all that would explain the stumpy tail. Then they would cross the road bridge that led them into and across the left hand-side of the village, up the windy hill parallel to the cascade, through the secured gate (as a council worker he possessed one of the few keys) and on to the footpath that ran across the top of the waterfall and so back into the territory of his own commune. For Charles and Milka, this was a secret place. Few people had a copy of the required key and even fewer of the select few ever bothered to take the path. For all intents and purposes the path and the surrounding scrub and low woodland was the *de facto* property of Charles and his dog.

In the year after Charles and Milka were united, November 11th fell on a Thursday meaning that the national government declared a so-called *'pont'* or bridging holiday to cover both the Thursday and the Friday. The Unions representing the French civil service are nothing if not inventive and so, many years previously, had pushed the Socialist government of the time to declare the *pont* if a public holiday should fall on either a Tuesday (giving also the Monday off) or, as in this case, the Thursday. Effectively, civil servants enjoy an extra-long weekend for two out of every five public holidays. In contrast, most people in the private sector are happy to celebrate Armistice Day of the First World War with a single day off while our overworked functionaries receive a well-deserved second day of paid vacation. The only losers in our Village (the one to the right of the cascade that is) was the poor *Fifine* who lost her most important and faithful clients for two full days.

As luck would have it, November 11th was a warm, sunny almost balmy day with the temperature creeping into the very low 20s. Charles' wife was not going to be fobbed off with any excuses on this public holiday and so convinced Charles to reserve a table at an upmarket restaurant in Annecy for lunch. Thus, once they had attended the commemorative ceremony at the village monument for those killed in action for *La Patrie* that took place at 11 am on the Eleventh Day of the Eleventh Month, they drove the twenty-odd kilometres to the restaurant leaving a moping and far from happy Milka back at home.

After what Charles considered a rather frugal and overpriced lunch, they drove back to their home. On the way, Charles queried his wife, on at least three separate occasions, how a squiggle of some coloured gel on the edge of the plate can turn a simple piece of terrine accompanied by a salad leaf into a seventeen-euro delicacy. And how could two baby carrot and a minced courgette thingamabob covered in aspic accompanying a small leg of chicken be sold for forty-five euros? And, even worse, how can a bottle of Savoie red costing only eight euros fifty centimes at the *vignoble* be sold for thirty euros in the restaurant? His wife had tried to reply logically but in the end stopped that topic of conversation by replying simply that he had just paid the price of '*la nouvelle cuisine*'!

Milka was of course awaiting their arrival and started barking in pleasure as soon as she heard the car doors close. As they entered she did her usual whirling dervish imitation, completely ignoring Charles' wife, and then went to the table in the hallway and came back with her leash held firmly in her mouth. This she dropped with well-practiced skill on to Charles' feet. Hint, hint!

After being teased by his wife that he had two women in his life and the younger one was much more impatient than the older one, he clipped Milka's lead on to her collar and they followed their usual procession: a quick pee (for Milka of course) on the scrawny patch of grass by the cascade; over the road that bridged the stream; quick march through the left hand commune; up the hill; passage through the locked gate and along the footpath that ran over the top of the cascade. Once the gate had been locked securely behind them, Charles released Milka's leash allowing the young dog to run off looking for a stick to bring to Charles so that he could throw it for her and continue her preferred, game *ad infinitum*. However,

Milka was a well-trained dog (apart from the whining) and never wandered far from Charles; certainly never letting him get too far out of her field of vision.

Charles invariably sat on a log that he had deliberately moved to the middle of the clearing where Milka played and patiently watched his canine friend as she enjoyed freedom from the leash and the exercise that came with running unhindered through the countryside.

On hearing a loud squawking from far overhead, he looked up and saw close to eighty large birds, certainly continental Cranes, flying in V-formation and honking for all they were worth as they flew across France and onwards towards Spain and warmer climes for the winter. As he gently stroked Milka's ear, he muttered that with weather like today, the cranes should have stayed around a little longer. In canine response, Milka brought him her stick, assuming (wrongly) that Charles wanted to continue to play their throw and fetch game.

The afternoon sun began to slide towards the ground off to his left telling Charles that they should be thinking of getting home before the sunlight was totally lost and the cool of the evening began to descend. As he threw Milka's stick for the final time for today, something odd happened: rather than chase after her stick, Milka was concentrating on what Charles took to be a small bird that was almost hovering in the air in front and over the top of them. When he looked more carefully after adjusting his spectacles, he realised that this was no bird but in fact a bat, a very small one, a Pipistrelle if his memory served him correctly. The Pipistrelle was soon joined by another and then another as they darted in their sightless flight in the air around Charles. Curious at this unexpected vision; after all it would soon be mid-November, he called Milka to heel and held her collar so that she would stop moving around and perhaps scare the bats. As soon as the pair were still, the pipistrelles, one after the other, swooped done and disappeared behind a tall clump of grass that grew out of a small, gently sloping bank.

"Now where did they go?" he asked himself. And being all the more curious, Charles stepped across to the clump of grass, searched around and finally discovering a small hole, not much bigger than his fist, that he assumed a curious rabbit or a hunting stoat must have dug at some time in the past. It could only have been into that hole that the bats had flown, there was no other option nearby that he could find.

Now, you or I or almost anyone else for that matter would have perhaps said "curious" and walked off, soon forgetting the evening observation. But not Charles. Do not forget that we are in the presence of a former international speleologist. What flashed through Charles excited mind and brought a flush of anticipation was the thought of a single word 'cave'. But he quickly decided that he could do nothing further today in the rapidly fading late-afternoon light. Better to get prepared for tomorrow; thank goodness for *le pont* on Friday and the weekend to follow that.

The following morning, soon after he heard the cockerels start to crow and while his wife was still softly snoring on her side of the bed, he took his clothes from the previous day off the bedroom chair and carried them into the bathroom across the landing. Milka followed closely behind. Once dressed, Milka fed and a flask of coffee prepared, Charles took his keys, unlocked the barn on the side of the house that served as his workshop and piled into his wheelbarrow a shovel, a mattock, a trowel, a crowbar, a metal picket, a club hammer, a winch, a length of strong nylon rope, a ball of twine and a couple of clean jute sacks. 'I don't think I'm forgetting anything,' he thought to himself as he picked up a stout torch, extra batteries and his caving helmet. But then had a second thought ... he put his phone in his pocket and then quickly scribbled a note to his wife telling her where he was going and including the words 'I think I have discovered an unknown cave above the waterfall!'.

At this early hour, the morning was chill but his excitement was such that he felt nothing but euphoria. He made his way as rapidly as possible along the now familiar route, being slowed by the need to keep the implements from toppling out of the wheelbarrow. Milka, in her impatience, ran ahead to her favourite patch of scrawny grass in front of the waterfall to relieve her overnight bladder. This early in the morning no one else was about and very few houses in the village (to the left of the waterfall) had any lights showing.

"Good," thought Charles, "less people to pester me for an explanation of what I am doing outside at such an early hour, and with a wheelbarrow full of tools."

He really wanted to keep the curious away, at least until he was sure about the cave.

They quickly mounted the hill leading to the locked gate, went through it, with Charles remembering to lock the gate behind him, and on to their well-trodden path. He used his seat, or rather log, as a first position-finder, then the clump of grass, and he soon rediscovered the small, fist-sized hole that was at the origin of all his excitement.

But first things first: a quick cup of coffee to get him fully awake and a food treat for Milka in the form of a length of dried bovine ligament (yuk, but she loved chewing on them!).

Charles had decided to start his excavations carefully. After all, the cave might be nothing more than a small depression; perhaps only a metre deep that would be sufficiently large to offer a safe haven for the Pipistrelles but not large enough to be an exciting discovery for him. And, if so, he did not want to destroy the bats' roost to satisfy his own curiosity. First he ran his hand over the surface of the ground where he would start his trial excavation and picked up all the larger pieces of rock and moved them well away from his work zone. Next, he brushed all the smaller stones off to the side and then folded the two jute sacks in four and carefully laid them in front of the hole. These were to be his kneeling pads and would protect his sensitive knees; especially the right one where he had been operated. He started off with an ordinary garden trowel and gently dug around the top of the hole. The soil crumbled as he pulled the sinuous grass roots away and the hole doubled in size as he used his other hand to scoop out the loose soil and push it to his left. After working carefully for fifteen minutes or so, he had before him a rabbit-sized hole that did not seem to vary much with depth as it disappeared at slightly more than a forty-five-degree angle into the earth, at least that is, as far as he could see in the still half-light of early morning.

He switched on his torch and shone it into the hole and could then see perhaps two metres down into the soil but no further. There appeared to be a block at the bottom of the hole.

At that point, many less curious people might have stopped their travails with the thought that the cave was merely the size of the hole that Charles was reviewing in the torchlight. His mind, however, was quickly considering the alternatives. For example, where are the bats since there are none roosting in the entire space he had revealed? Well, perhaps they are still outside, OK, but then where was their guano, their mouse-like droppings? At least some trace of bat dung should be visible in the lamp light. Charles' mind reasoned that if there were no bats roosting in the hole and no significant traces of their droppings then he could not yet have reached their roosting site. This to his excited mind then told him that the hole (or rather the cave) must be more extensive than his torch was revealing. There was only one way to find out if his theory was correct: keep digging!

Charles' next problem to solve was how could he get to the bottom of the rabbit hole-sized passage in order to check for and eventually remove any blockage at the bottom that, just might, lead into a cave gallery. Well, only one way really and that was to go inside. However, while he was relatively slim, he did have a *bidon* (beer tummy) from drinking rather too much alcohol *Chez-Fifine* and there was no way he, or most other adults could push their way down the twenty-centimetre-wide hole without getting stuck like a cork in a bottle … and, furthermore, he would be obliged to go down head first with his arms extended in front for digging. His only solution was therefore to make the entrance hole and then the down-shaft to the assumed blockage rather larger, at least as large as an adult male could easily descend without fear of getting stuck tight.

He put the garden trowel back in the wheelbarrow and carried the crowbar and mattock over to the hole. A couple of gentle swings of the mattock at the top of the entrance hole was sufficient to convince Charles that he was faced with a solid limestone barrier. No go in that area then, but the barrier provided the silver lining in that the top of the passageway was unlikely to subside inwards, always a danger to cavers and potholers. Next he swung his mattock at the base of the entrance hole, the soil gave easily allowing him to clear a considerably wider space and slowly open up the diameter of the entrance hole. Little by little he pulled soil and rocks out of the small but expanding tunnel in front of him, sometimes needing to use the crowbar to wedge out any rocks that got in his way or simply using his hands to shovel the soil to the front of the hole where he pushed it to one side. From time to time he was obliged to stop the excavation and shovel the accumulating soil into his wheelbarrow and move it away from the entrance.

At first, he could only lay on the sacks with his head, now wearing his safety helmet with an incorporated miner's lantern to provide a more intense light, just inside the hole and his arms stretched out in front to dig and then shovel out earth as he worked on the floor of the tunnel. By the time the church clock struck midday, only his legs from the knees down would have been visible to any curious passerby. At one o'clock in the afternoon, it was only his boot clad feet that were visible. Perhaps time to take a break he thought; better even to go home for lunch and declare himself still alive to his ever patient wife; and he was rather hungry after skipping breakfast this morning.

Milka announced their arrival home with one of her trademark yaps and a rapid beating of her six-vertebrae tail. As they entered the front door, with Charles stopping to remove his boots and rather dirty anorak, his wife called out a cheery greeting; something about the returning Neanderthal and his wolf assistant! French humour, no less, but stimulating a quick laugh from Charles-the-Caveman.

After rapidly eating (actually his wife thought gobbling) his lunch and doing the washing up, Charles gave his wife a quick peck on the cheek and told her that he would see her tonight unless she wished to stop past the dig to see his progress this afternoon.

As Charles walked back towards his newly discovered cave, his mind was in overdrive on the question of how he should now proceed with the next stage of his excavations. What had really caused him to take a break for lunch was the fact that he appeared to have gone as far as he could in digging, excavating and widening the downwards directed rabbit hole he had discovered thanks to the bats. Now he appeared to have reached a block in the tunnel; perhaps a large stone or boulder of the native limestone. Because of the absence of bats and guano in the initial tunnel, he knew that there must be a way through, albeit currently small, to another gallery, but how and even could he get through to such a gallery? After all, bats may need only a hole of five or six centimetres to pass through but an adult human wearing a thick anorak would require a space of at least forty centimetres in diameter. The other unknown that concerned him was, supposing he actually could get through the block, what awaited him on the other side? Would the slope of the initial tunnel continue at its current, rather gentle angle akin to an infant's slide, would it perhaps even-off, or, more perilously, would there be a gaping drop underneath? Charles had no idea and so prudence had to be the order of the day; especially as he was working on his own. For these reasons, once back to the hole, he took the metal picket and used the club hammer to drive it into the ground at a metre distant from the hole. To the picket he attached the nylon rope and ran this through a simple winch, then tied the rope around his waist. He was now ready to try his first means of removing that blockage.

Holding on to the end of the rope, Charles allowed himself gently to slide into the hole, feet first, slowly playing out rope as he descended until he reached the bottom of the hole. He tried stamping first one foot and then the other in this initial attempt to remove the blockage; nothing doing!

"OK", he thought, "I need to use a bigger gun to tackle this blockage" and so he winched himself back out of the hole, collected the crowbar and the club hammer and re-entered the hole, this time head first with his arms outstretched in front of him. In his left hand he held the club hammer with the right gripping tightly on to the crowbar. He lay the hammer at the bottom of the hole freeing both hands to prod away at the base of the small tunnel. Initially, he only made contact with rock but as he worked his way around the edges of the blockage, he began to find the softer resistance of packed soil. Little by little, in the confined space, he prodded at the soil slowly progressing around the edges of the rock barrier, occasionally picking up the hammer to strike the top of the crowbar to remove a particularly stubborn stone. Fully forty minutes after beginning this phase of his work, the blockage started, at first, to move slowly downwards and then, with a rush, it disappeared into a prolongation of the tunnel. Its final noise being a loud plop as it must have landed in water lying somewhere below followed by another, smaller plop as the club hammer followed marginally behind. Only the rope tied judiciously around his waist prevented Charles from continuing the same trajectory as the stone and his hammer.

"Thank the Lord," Charles thought, "now on to the next stage," as he winched himself carefully downwards to see what lay below.

His rabbit hole or entrance tunnel now appeared to measure around five or six metres in depth and he could see in the light of his helmet the club hammer and the rock that had caused the original blockage. Both hammer and rock lay in a puddle of water; nothing too deep to worry about. But oddly, the rock appeared to glisten in the light of his lamp. He knew immediately why this was but at the same time he was surprised by his observation.

He continued to feed out rope so that he slowly descended until his outstretched hand came in contact first with the water and then with the rocky base of the cave. A little more rope and he was able to gently lower himself on to the floor of the cave, turn around and stand on his feet. He had arrived!

He now turned his attention back to the rock that had provided the initial barrier and scrutinised it closely with his light. As he had seen before, the rock twinkled from numerous places where he knew metallic intrusions and perhaps quartz were showing at the surface of the granite rock. It was the metallic intrusions in particular that were reflecting his lamplight. Nothing unusual about that or about the granitic parent rock except, except that the bedrock in this area of Savoie was purely limestone and the nearest granite outcrops lay over one hundred kilometres away in Switzerland. How on earth then could the rock have gotten all the way here? Charles decided to think about this anomaly at a later date as he rolled the stone out of his path. Now for some exploring!

But first things first. Exploring a new cave was always risky, even dangerous: getting lost in a new cave during exploration was the simplest thing to do while having an accident and needing to be rescued was putting the potential rescuers at risk too. Charles winched himself out of the tunnel, walked to the wheelbarrow and picked up the ball of twine. He attached the end to the metal picket and started to unwind the ball as he backed towards the hole. Milka seeing where her owner was going, beat him to it and gracefully slid down the hole and plopped into the puddle at the bottom of the slope. Thankfully, Charles had thought to move the granite boulder.

"Oh well, dog, if you want to come caving too, I should at least make sure you are comfortable," and he picked up one of the jute sacks before re-entering the tunnel and sliding gently to the bottom.

As he went, he unwound the twine ensuring that he was leaving a trail behind that he could follow to ensure his safe exit from the cave; just like in Theseus and the Minotaur (without the Minotaur, he hoped, of course!). The first part of Charles' exploration took him along a low rocky tunnel that had a few centimetres of water along its length. The tunnel, while wide enough for Milka to walk along was much too low for Charles, even if he hunched right over. The only way to proceed was by crawling on all fours. This new part of the tunnel was flat, continued into the earth for about ten metres before taking a sharp left turn. Milka, disappeared from his lamplight as she took the turn ahead of him. Charles called out to her to wait for him as he continued to crawl along behind, cursing the chilly water that was soaking into the front of his clothes. This minor inconvenience was forgotten as soon as he turned the corner and his lamp played over the scene in front of him; what a magnificent sight awaited its first viewing by modern man; perhaps by any humanoid.

The cave he entered was fully thirty metres deep and at least that wide; an enormous cavern that would compete with some of the largest in Savoie, even in the whole of France. But what was even more impressive, revealed by his wandering lamplight, was the height of the cavern that rose at least seven or eight metres above his head; a cathedral of a monument to nature's power and beauty.

Growing down from the roof of the cavern, like stone icicles, were several majestic stalactites while seeming to sprout up from the floor were an equal number of impressive stalagmites, at least three of them probably taller than himself. But the most stunning view was near to the centre of the cavern where a stalagmite and a stalactite had merged to form a single, massive column as if deliberately placed to hold up the roof of this, his, subterranean edifice. Charles' cave.

It was at this moment that Charles realised that Milka was at his feet, looking up at her master, perhaps mystified by the awe he was exuding in this mysterious place. He noticed that she was shaking, perhaps in fear, perhaps due to the coolness of the cavern, perhaps due to the cold water that she had wandered through in her passage along the tunnel. In his lamplight he noticed a ridge of soil raised about a metre off the floor and on to this he laid the sack. He called to Milka to jump up and then to lie down. She obeyed immediately and, after a few moments of turning around and sniffing, Charles noticed that his dog had fallen asleep on the sacking that, of course, bore his odour from this morning's work.

Charles placed the ball of twine next to Milka and continued with hands free to explore in the lamplight. On two occasions he realised why cavers and underground workers, like miners, always wear protective headgear as his helmet scrapped against down dips of the cave roof. Without the helmet he would have received serious scalp wounds; a fate that frequently awaits the reckless and inexperienced 'Sunday' cave explorers. Once across to the other side of the large chamber, Charles found that the roof of the cavern rapidly decreased and narrowed into another small tunnel where, once more, he realised that he would need to crawl to see what lay on the other side. Being too risky to take this tunnel without the ball of twine to show him the way back, he quickly re-crossed the cavern, picked up the twine and again began to unroll it behind him as he retraced his steps to the entrance to the new tunnel. Here he dropped to his knees and then on to his stomach and begin to crawl along the narrow passageway leading away from the large chamber. He crawled for fully three minutes on a gentle downward slope; indicating to his experienced mind a distance of between fifteen to twenty metres. As he crawled, he noted other tunnels leading off first to the right and then to the left. These he would need to explore later but for now he continued straight on. Finally, he came to the end of the tunnel and emerged into a smaller room-like chamber of perhaps twenty-five square metres ... and received yet another shock. There, at the end of this new chamber, stood a large, irregular-shaped block of granite like a giant's table or an altar. Using elongated steps, he measured the block as being around three metres long by four metres deep and at least another three metres high. A block of solid granite, that he reminded himself must have hailed from Switzerland. This block of some thirty-five to forty cubic metres and therefore weighing up to one hundred tons, was now sitting inside a cave where he had been obliged to crawl on his stomach to gain entrance. He knew that it must have been transported from Switzerland by the force of a glacier at least ten thousand years ago, but perhaps, just perhaps, far, far earlier in prehistory. But the timing was not the issue, what puzzled him was how it had managed to find its way inside to this point in the cave system. Somewhere there must be an enormous entrance still waiting to be discovered. Clearly more secrets were to be revealed by this cave; but not today.

Charles remembered to take photos with his mobile phone of this final (for today at least) chamber and did a reasonable selfie to show the sheer size of the 'Giant's Altar' – as he now named the block of granite – before crawling back along the tunnel and into the 'Cathedral Cavern'. Here he took another series of photos particularly of the large stalactites and stalagmites and the central pillar before starting to rewind the ball of twine. After crossing the chamber, Charles gently stroked Milka's back and received a welcoming lick on his hand in response. Since her sleeping shelf seemed to have remained bone dry, he decided to leave the folded sack in place thinking that will do for Milka tomorrow.

Together they retraced their steps and when they arrived at the 'Rabbit Hole' entrance and could see the afternoon light, Milka scrambled up the slope with Charles following rather more slowly behind. Once outside in the late afternoon air, he suddenly realised just how tired he felt.

On arriving home, first things first, Charles telephoned through to *M. le Maire* and reported his discovery of the new cave system. They arranged a visit together the following morning, despite it being the weekend. He also telephoned through to an old friend who was the president of his old speleological club in Annecy and received a promise also to be present the following day, accompanied by another, senior club member. Once the phone was back in its cradle, Charles could then turn to his wife, kiss her gently on the lips and show her the photos he had taken in the newly discovered *"Grotte de la Cascade"* as he now named the cave above the waterfall. His wife was impressed by what his work of a single day had achieved. "Well done Charles, my love," she said before making him a cup of tea and handing across a plate of biscuits.

The following day, Charles led a small expedition comprised of *M. le Maire*, his two caving buddies and Milka-the-dog. He carried with him a spare helmet for the *Maire* and the usual bag of safety products containing a small first aid kit, spare torches, batteries and the ball of twine. On arrival at the cave, Charles explained about the seeing the bats, then about the descent down the enlarged rabbit hole, receiving – as he knew he would – considerable teasing from his caving friends. One asked if this was the Bat Cave of the super-hero while the other wanted to know if he was Alice, the March Hare or perhaps even the White Rabbit himself! But the mayor chimed in with the observation that by looking at Charles' face, he would think rather the Cheshire Cat!

Teasing over, his two colleagues slid, one after the other, gently down the incline before calling upwards "next".

"After you, *M. le Maire*", offered Charles to the by now greenish-looking face of his commune's elected officer. "It's quite safe and my two friends are waiting to catch you below."

While the mayor hesitated, Milka took the plunge down the hole instead, which steadied the mayor's nerves sufficiently, that he sat on the slope and cried "weeee ..." as he slid down into the grasp of one of the speleologists waiting below.

Charles followed closely behind and then led them along the same route as the previous day and into the Cathedral Cavern. Everyone stood quietly in awe of the scene that they were witnessing in the combined lights of their torches. Meanwhile, Milka already bored, jumped up on to her ledge and promptly fell asleep on the jute sack. Charles' friends began to take measurements and notes. They worked initially with an electronic measuring device that most people see operating in the hands of estate agents. As one measured, the other took notes. Once the three main dimensions of the cave were recorded, they began to take further measurements of the size and positions of the larger stalactites and stalagmites. Their detailed dossier was completed by a series of photographs taken on a proper caving camera; no mobile phones to be used here!

They then followed the tunnel leading to the Giant's Altar and stood back and waited for *M. le Maire* (a university professor of Geology) to understand the significance of this find. It did not take long for him to utter an unprintable phrase that ended with the remark "how did that massive block of granite arrive here from Switzerland?"

"Carried in a glacier ..." offered one of Charles' friends.

"Yes, of course, but I mean HERE, inside this cave. Clearly there had to have been an entrance large enough for the block to have been carried into the cave. All I can suggest is that either there is another entrance that Charles has not yet discovered or a rockfall has sealed another entrance, perhaps for good. But what a find Charles, what an enigma, congratulations, *mon vieux.*"

M. le Maire then decided that this would be a good moment to leave, after all he had other official functions to perform this weekend, including inaugurating a new fire engine followed by an invitation to lunch with the *Pétanque* Players Association (to which he gave a generous commune handout) followed in the afternoon by chairing the environmental committee. For this last act he and his fellow committee members would receive handsome tax-free re-munerations in the guise of *'jetons de présence'* (or a 'bums-on-seats' reward) for doing their elected jobs.

Well, you can believe me that it did not take long for the word to get around. *M. le Maire,* ever keeping a watchful eye on his slim electoral majority made calls to the departmental Prefect, the member of parliament (or *Député*) of his circumscription and then, with less fanfare, to the editor of the X-Times newspaper. Within two days, the newspaper carried stunning photos of the inside of the cave system under garish headlines copying the Alice in Wonderland theme. The photos came neither from Charles' camera nor those of his caving friends, so someone must have gone back into the cave system unannounced ...

The X-Times article was then picked up by larger newspapers, ensuring the notoriety of the commune (to the right of the cascade) and multiple requests for Charles to give interviews and lead journalistic expeditions around the newly discovered cave system.

A more scientific report was to appear eight months later in the European Journal of Speleology, co-authored by Charles and his caving friends.

Meanwhile, during the time that the Mayor was inaugurating the fire engine and taking lunch with the commune's *pétanque* players; the three cavers explored the side tunnels that had been revealed to Charles during his initial afternoon of discovery. None of these three tunnels revealed very much of additional interest but the cavers did note the accumulation of considerable soil at the end of one of them – suggesting an area that they might explore in the future. This was also close to the roosting spot of the pipistrelle colony that had started all the fun and that had led to Charles' discovery.

As months and then years went by, first public interest and then scientific interest in the cave system inevitably waned. But not for Charles; two years after his initial discovery of the cave system, he took retirement and this allowed him additional time to continue to explore, dig and photograph the inside of the caves. He even took a metal detector with him on one occasion thinking that perhaps early Bronze or Iron Age man might have made use of the cave system and left metallic objects behind; but this search was in vain. He also started to excavate the soil from behind the Giant's Altar to see whether the lost entrance might be positioned there but his digging only lasted a single day because a more careful check of the relevant and large-scale ordonnance survey map showed that the mountain stream that fed the cascade likely ran only thirty or forty metres away, and above, from where he believed the Giant's Altar stood. Getting drowned in his discovery would not be the best way of leaving his work for future generations!

On his trips underground, he was of course always accompanied by Milka and she invariably took residence on her ledge that now contained three or four folded jute sacks to ensure her comfort. She was getting older too. He now made fewer and fewer guided tours; partly because of waning interest and partly because he was becoming more possessive of his discovery. The final straw to volunteering to lead small tour groups came when a teacher at the local primary school wanted to bring a group of eight eleven-year-olds to visit; whatever next? The last request convinced him to pull down his guide shutters and allow interest from potential visitors to wane even further. Eventually, people in the local area began to forget about *la Grotte de la Cascade*.

Sadly, not everyone had forgotten because, late one Monday afternoon, soon after Charles' seventy-first birthday, he received a call from the local *gendarmerie* based in a neighbouring commune. The sergeant at the other end of the telephone asked Charles if he would confirm that he was the gentleman who had discovered the cave system above the Cascade and, when Charles replied in the affirmative, the gendarme asked if he would not mind coming to the police station. 'Curious,' thought Charles as he took his coat and car keys, closely followed by Milka, and drove the twelve kilometres to the *gendarmerie*.

On arrival in the parking of the small police station, Charles noticed a large van with Swiss 'VD' number plates parked next to a police station wagon. People from Geneva, he deduced.

Once inside the building, he introduced himself to the desk officer and was immediately taken to a room located behind the officer's desk. A quick knock and Charles entered. On one side of the table sat two gendarmes in uniform including the station's lieutenant, and on the other side sat three men in rather muddy clothes. The lieutenant stood up and asked Charles to follow him. They went back outside and across to the Swiss registered van. The police officer opened the back doors and there, lying on thick layers of bubble wrap were three long stalagmites that had been cleanly cut presumably by the angle grinder that sat next to them and in front of what looked like a small portable generator.

"My men stopped the van earlier this afternoon during a routine check and noticed how muddy the men's clothes were so they asked them to open the back doors of the van. When my gendarmes questioned what the 'stones' were in the back of the van and where they came from, the Swiss guys told a fancy story about having bought them from an antique dealer. When queried in which town was located the supposed antique dealer, the Swiss mentioned a town where we know for a fact that there are no such dealers; honest or dishonest. This raised my men's suspicions sufficiently that they brought them back here for further questioning. I happened to remember that several years ago there was an article about you finding the cavern above the cascade and subsequently you kindly showed me around the cave system. The reason that I asked you to come this evening was to seek confirmation that the blocks in the back of the van are not stones taken from a ruin somewhere but in fact stalagmites. If so, this is a serious crime."

"They most certainly are stalagmites; look how they are thick at the base and narrow upwards. I have heard in the past about the traffic of such objects because first of all they are very ancient, perhaps over twenty thousand years in the formation, and second, being composed of pure lime or calcite, they polish up rather well and can be used as large room decorations. I have seen such objects in castles in Romania and also in large homes in Asia. And I presume that is the reason these men have cut the stalagmites destroying so many years of nature's work. Did they say where they came from?"

"Not yet," replied the lieutenant but they will not leave the station until they do. Thanks for coming so promptly, thanks for your help and I will not keep you further."

As he drove away from the police station, Charles had that feeling of dread that I imagine we have all felt at some time in our lives. Rather than go straight home to explain to his wife why the police had wanted his presence, he drove immediately to the hillside above the waterfall, parking badly by the side of the gate. He remembered to grab his caving helmet from the back seat of the car and let Milka out of the side door.

His instinctive feeling of fear was confirmed when he saw the gate standing wide open, and he could see straight away that the gated entrance had been crowbarred open. He ran as fast as his seventy-odd year old legs would carry him and went straight down the rabbit hole pulling on his helmet and switching on the light as soon as he reached the bottom. Milka followed closely behind. He crawled along the tunnel and arrived in the Cathedral Cavern. There was no doubt; the Swiss had neatly sectioned three of the most magnificent stalagmites. Tears bubbled up in Charles' eyes and all he could say was "no, please, no." But too late, the damage was done.

Really feeling his age, he slowly clambered up the slope and out of the rabbit hole and made his way back to his car, trying futilely to close the damaged gate properly behind him.

He arrived back home and, between heart wrenching sobs, told his wife a potted version of the story. Milka quietly lay across his feet, just as she had done as a puppy, obviously understanding his sorrow. When he had appeared to calm down and the sobs had quietened, his wife told him to relax, breathe deeply and that she would go to the kitchen to fetch them both a hefty cognac.

Three minutes later she returned to the sitting room holding the two glasses in her hands. She found Charles slumped in his armchair with eyes staring upwards.

The funeral was held in the commune's little church and the ceremony officiated by the priest who covered several local parishes. The church was packed, mostly of course with local friends and neighbours who came to pay their respects but also by around a dozen of his former caving friends who arrived from Annecy and Aix-les-Bains in two minibuses. The police lieutenant was also present, sitting near the front of the church and feeling rather guilty. Journalists from the X-Times and a larger departmental paper who had been informed of the ceremony by *M. le Maire* were present to keep their readers abreast of the latest local news.

Charles widow left home to walk to the church – she wanted none of the limousine on offer. As she opened her front door, she remembered that she had left her black hat in the kitchen and went back to collect it, leaving the front door slightly ajar. In the short time that she needed to collect her hat, Milka had slipped out the door.

The ceremony was sad, as such events inevitably are. The presidents of both the Aix-les-Bains and the Annecy Speleological

Associations both made speeches about what a loss Charles was to the caving fraternity. Many in the audience had no idea that their friend and neighbour was so recognised in his field. *M. le Maire* spoke eloquently about 'his friend Charles' who had followed his dream and discovered *la Grotte de la Cascade,* a cave system that was in pristine condition until *les trois Suisse,* in parody to a clothes catalogue, came and cut down nature's splendour. The final speech was a dual effort made by Gé-Gé and Henri to their former colleague and dear friend. But neither were able to finish their handwritten speeches with first Henri bursting into tears which infected Gé-Gé as he tried to finish his note of respect.

After the church ceremony, Charles' coffin was taken to the local cemetery where his remains were lowered carefully into the hole dug in his family plot. One of his caving friends said a few words out loud to the people who had gathered at the graveside. Among his tender words was the remark that while most of us fear the moment that we will be placed in the ground, this was never an issue for Charles, apart from his loving family, being underground was his passion.

His wife, their two children and tiny grandchildren each dropped a red rose onto his coffin before the priest said a final prayer for the departed and the entourage walked sadly out of the graveyard. The wake for Charles was held, of course, *Chez Fifine* and, before the proceedings broke up, a by now rather elderly *La Fifine* led a final toast to the 'gentle soul that we have lost'.

Charles' family then went back to their quiet home and tried to talk through their sadness by reciting incidents and their humorous moments from Charles' life. It was as Charles' son mentioned the sadness that his dad had experienced when his Advanced Potholing licence was not renewed and then the joy that he had experienced when they had brought Milka home to him that everyone said out aloud "but where is Milka?". This was the first moment that anyone had remarked her absence.

Milka was never to be found and her disappearance appeared to be an unsolvable mystery before the family slowly forgot about her.

In 1994, I was working at the *Mairie* helping the secretaries to file away a mass of old papers when I came across the notes written by our former mayor concerning the discovery of *la Grotte de la Cascade,* some twenty-five years previously. I read through the papers carefully and then made photocopies to take home with me. 'What an intriguing story' I thought to myself. Since the mayor of that time had thoughtfully dated the papers, I knew quite precisely when the cavern had been discovered. Next, I drove to the library of the nearest town and used one of their computers to search through digital copies of newspapers of that time. The first story I found was in a copy of the X-Times of late 1969 and a more detailed one from a national newspaper of early 1970. The photos showed the splendour of the Cathedral Cavern and the enigma of the Giant's Altar block of granite.

My next move was to call on the mayor of that time, now in his late eighties, and I found him exceptionally spry and with a perfect memory.

He told me the story of Charles and the discovery of the Bat Cave, as many people had nicknamed the cavern at that time. He gave me the details of the prosecution of the Swiss who had desecrated the cave by cutting down those three stalagmites, and the fact that their illegal act had caused poor Charles to suffer the intense shock that had led to his fatal stroke. Their penalty of six months suspended jail time paled into insignificance when the impact of their deed on poor Charles was considered.

Finally, the mayor told me that a week or two after Charles funeral he had ordered commune workers to erect a barred and lockable gate at the entrance to the cave. A barred rather than solid gate was chosen to allow entry of the pipistrelle bats to their subterranean roost. From that day on, no one had entered the cave, partly out of respect to Charles, partly because interest in the cave had started to wane and then be forgotten.

"*M. le Maire*, who now has the key to the gate?" I asked, "I would love to visit the cavern and appreciate just what Charles had discovered."

"The key? Oh, I think I must have a copy among my old papers." The long retired mayor left his sitting room and reappeared ten minutes later with a labelled keyring holding three keys. "Oh, Pierre-Antoine, it looks like I kept all the keys," he said handing them over to me. "I would love to come with you and revisit the caves but I think I am now a little too old to go down the rabbit-hole tunnel. But here are copies of the cavern plans that I also found in my papers. There is really no way to get lost but don't forget to wear a proper helmet and do take a good torch and some spare batteries with you."

The following morning, I collected the basic caving gear and followed the route that Charles must have taken so many times in the past; except the path was now very overgrown and I had to use secateurs to clip through straggling blackberry switches. I was accompanied by my father-in-law and my two children: my son aged eight and my twelve-year-old daughter. Our initial idea was that with my father-in-law present, each adult could be responsible for a child while we were inside the cave.

As the old mayor had predicted, the rabbit hole entrance was easily visible although the gate's locking device had gotten a little rusty but nothing that a quick spray of WD40 could not sort out.

Once the gate was opened, we each took turns to look down the rabbit hole using our torches. My father-in-law immediately declared that his tummy would be too large for him to descend the tunnel although I considered that it was probably more a question of his claustrophobia than his girth! He called my son over and told him that he should remain aboveground with him for the time being. Once his sister had looked around the cave with her dad, it would be his turn to go down the rabbit hole.

We put on our helmets, and I stepped backwards into the hole and gently slid down the slope landing feet first into the trickle of water that still existed at the bottom. My daughter then followed and then my son appeared too, rather too closely behind his sister.

"I didn't want to stay outside with *papy* so I followed you in," he declared.

Now we were all inside, we crawled along on our stomachs with the tunnel lit by our torches. I emerged first into the 'Cathedral Cavern' and picked out straightaway one of the stalagmites that had been chopped off. My daughter came over to stand next to me, and I explained how that act of vandalism had directly led to the death of the poor man who had discovered the cave system so many years before.

From immediately behind me I heard my eight-year-old call out "dad, what's this, can you see, look up there?"

I turned around and could see in his lamplight a shelf of soil, sitting perhaps a metre off the ground, and seemingly covered in some sort of rotting material. Lying on top of the material was a skeleton of quite a large animal:

We had discovered Milka who certainly died while patiently and lovingly awaiting Charles' return.

7 |

The Land of Four Half Elephants

PART 1
THE CRIMINAL

My name is Alioune Diouf and I come from a small village called Keur Bisarre on the outskirts of the Doli cattle ranch and very close to the ever-expanding metropolis of Touba in the Peanut Basin of Western Senegal. Touba is the most rapidly expanding city in West Africa and now has passed the greater Dakar conurbation in population and economic importance. However, while Touba is still geographically a part of Senegal, it is to all intents and purposes an independent state within the country. The usual national services do not operate here, there are no government taxes collected, social planning is centralised within Touba itself as is everything to do with town planning and building control and permission. Our town, the City-State-of-Touba, is governed by bodies owing only allegiance to the seniors of the Brotherhood and we, the simple folk, hold loyalty to our religious leaders far above any respect of the state. So rigorous is the hold of the Brotherhood on Touba and our religious laws, that a former president of Senegal, himself an elderly member of the Brotherhood, went on his knees to our leaders and sparked country-wide debate with our newspaper headlines asking: 'Is the President a *Talibé* or is the *Talibé* a President?' By way of explanation, the word '*talibé*' is usually understood to be a young student in a Koranic school but is, in reality, a religious disciple. When even the elected president of the country goes on his knees to our leaders, you can imagine their sway over the less important members of the population in the country.

In my young days, from the age of six years old, my father had sent me to receive instructions in the Holy Koran from a well-respected Koranic teacher in a small town neighbouring Touba. At such a young age, it was terrible to have to leave home and join the other small boys at the school. But, after the first few difficult weeks, we all settled in and made friends. My best friend and fellow *talibé* was a boy a year older than me called Matar Fall. So much did we resemble each other that many who did not know us thought that we must be brothers, if not twins. Matar is to form a central part of my story, as you will see.

Luck was on my side with the Koranic school that my father had chosen for me because our teacher proved a devout and honourable man. He took his role of instructing us in how to follow in the footsteps of The Prophet through careful teaching and instruction, very, very seriously. Yes, he was firm but he was never cruel and we were never, ever abused. We were disciplined when we were naughty but when we went out to collect '*Zakat*' (charity) he never once asked us to go out specifically to collect money, just food to help feed the other members of our school. In contrast, we heard some real horror stories from a few of the bigger boys of goings-on in some of the other schools they knew; goings-on that were not acceptable or compatible with our religion.

Our teacher, the Imam, was also considered modern because he insisted that in addition to our native Wolof and the Arabic of our religion, all the *talibé* must learn to speak and write French, the language of government and of commerce in our country. He knew that some of us would need that foreign language during our future working lives; luckily for Matar and me!

At the age of eleven and Matar being twelve, we left the Koranic school and went to a local French language school where we *'sort of studied.'* I, in particular, found the stories of French pomp and glory rather boring and maths even more so. After all what does a peasant boy from the peanut basin of Senegal care whether or not Napoleon won or lost the battle of Waterloo back in 1815? Come on, that was over two hundred years ago anyway, move on! History aside, I was not much better in maths except that I could always come up with a thousand places that Pythagoras could stick his right angles. Because of this flippancy, I was never very popular with the teachers of the school and so they were happy to see the back of me, aged fourteen.

What to do now? Easy, my father always needed extra hands to plough, plant and weed his peanut fields. At first I did not mind lending my dad a hand, along with my many brothers and sisters; working together was always a bit of a giggle. After all, my dad had three wives and they had collectively given birth to sixteen children, greedy no? At his peak, my dad managed to birth three babies in a single year and, as all those kids grew up, so there were almost always more hands to help in the fields than were really needed. But, of course, the flipside was that there were ever more mouths to be fed.

When I reached the age of sixteen and a few months, I started to see a pretty Wolof girl from the neighbouring town of Diourbel (Touba girls are strictly off limits unless you want a call from their dads, complete with cattle castrating equipment) while Matar was becoming increasingly friendly with her older sister. Life was fun, that is until Matar's girlfriend told him that a baby was on the way; unexpectedly.

When I asked Matar "what steps will you take my brother?"

He replied, between deep guffaws, "very big ones, bro. I'm off to Dakar, want to come? I have no intention of getting married. Who knows if the baby is even mine?"

With that decision made, and with a few thousand CFA between us in our pockets, we left very early in the morning without saying a word to our families, carrying our bags containing the few clothes we possessed to the local truck stop. Our luck was in because a fully laden truck was parked up and we could see the driver walking back after visiting the public latrine.

Our request for a lift was accepted with a sole condition: we should help to unload the lorry on arrival in Dakar. Deal done we squeezed into the cab and were soon underway, destination the big city and capital. And, by the way, those sacks of peanuts, as it turned out, were bloody heavy; forty kilograms each ... and there were a lot of them stuffed on the truck!

No matter, by early afternoon we had finished and were invited to share a simple meal of white rice and a small piece of the sardine-like yaabooy fish; tasty but full of bones. As we finished up this rather frugal meal, the friendly truck driver asked where we were now going and where we planned to spend the night. Of course we had absolutely no idea.

"Listen, you boys are from Touba and you might know that Dakar has a big contingent of '*Baye Fall*' operating in the town, why not search them out, for example on the Island of Gorée; I'm sure they can help you find somewhere to stay."

And that is exactly what we did, spending a couple of hundred CFA each to get to the Dakar Port and take a ferry over to the island to meet up with the *Baye Fall* or the 'Brotherhood Army of True Believers'. These young guys, theoretically as we were to find out, have sworn against any material possessions and thus live uniquely by begging. They have always been easily recognisable by the very bright blue and white striped clothes that they wear, often sporting dreadlocks (and so sometimes confused by tourists as Rastafarians – which they most certainly are not). They operate in small groups, are noisy, and frequently harass tourists in their quest for alms. Another fact about certain of the *Baye Fall* (you will not find this in the literature) and which is always denied by any serious member of the Brotherhood, is that they frequently do whatever they please!

Once we were well integrated into the *Baye Fall*, a rapid and easy task given our origins in Touba, we began to discover that our community consisted of two diametrically opposite halves. While most of the group followed the strict rules laid down by our founder, quite a few of the youngsters undertook activities that would be condemned by our leaders in Touba; if only they knew. Particularly relaxed in their behaviour was most of our band gathered on Gorée. Their forbidden pleasures included the frequent smoking of hashish and the drinking alcohol. They also loved to chase after any young tourist lady who showed any interest in their cheeky behaviour and tried to convince them to fall for their undoubted charms. As they told me on many occasions 'fornication rules, OK'?

After my rather sheltered life in the peanut basin, it did not take me long to appreciate these unexpected side-lines of our new life. And there lay my downfall and the real start of my adventures.

Six months after arrival on Gorée, I awoke one morning in a small hotel room that overlooked the port where the ferry from Dakar arrives every thirty minutes during the day. On the bedside table to my left were the remains of two fat reefers sitting in an ashtray plus an almost empty bottle of Scotch. To my right was a spotty, fake blond German woman that I vaguely remembered chatting with the evening before but precious little else.

The fact that we were both naked under the light sheet and the clear evidence provided by the Johnny Walker and the pair of some of the best Gorée Snuffs told me all I needed to know. Obviously the room was not mine, I had no room to speak of, and so the young lady must have brought me back to her room. Well, any healthy male of just sixteen after a good night's sleep would do what I did: I reached a hand over the woman's shoulder and gently caressed her breasts. The response was not what I had anticipated for she sat up stiffly, looked at me in fright and started to scream as though she had woken up in a cemetery. She continued screaming for the next five minutes and nothing I could say or do would calm her down. Finally, her door burst open and a burly French guy, I assumed he was the hotel owner or manager, walked through the door. He was followed by three local lads still wearing their waiter outfits and, just to complete the reception committee, there were also three French military-types in uniform who happened to be at the hotel having their breakfast. 'Here's trouble,' I remembered thinking!

I was allowed to go into the en-suite bathroom to put my *Baye Fall* clothes back on and then frog-marched by the two resident Gorée gendarmes to their holding cell. An hour later, despite the best attempts of Matar and other friends from our group to get me released, I was taken across on the ferry and locked up in the large prison at the port. I was left alone and worrying for several hours before I received my first visitor who introduced himself as Detective Inspector Touré. 'Blast,' I remembered thinking, 'he's a Peulh and likely a Tijane and most certainly not a member of the Brotherhood, so unlikely to be very sympathetic to a *Baye Fall* like me. I am in some deep *kaka*!'

The detective asked me to relate my story and not to leave anything out. As I spoke, so an assistant wrote down the contents of the interview. At just sixteen and of course relatively naïve in life, I thought best to tell the truth, and so I did.

I told them "I remembered the girl coming over to my group in the early evening. All of us were interested because she was wearing very short shorts and a clingy halter top. She was very provocative, especially to this *ky-ky* (our slang for a peasant). We chatted for a short while, I vaguely remembered swigging from a bottle of whisky but after that, all was blank until the events of this morning."

The Inspector nodded and allowed his scribe to finish writing out my words before saying that he had interviewed the girl and she claimed that you had drugged and then raped her. A doctor has examined her and confirmed recent sexual intercourse. He also took a sample of her blood and has found traces of GHB.

"What is GHB," I asked, "are you telling me she has a venereal disease?"

The scribe laughed aloud and received, in return, a hard stare from the inspector. "No GMB or gamma hydroxybutyric acid is the so-called 'date-rape' drug and we suspect that you added it to the whisky bottle. We have found traces in the dregs of alcohol in the bottle too. This is looking very serious young man but before charging you formally, I will give you a last chance to admit everything to us."

"I am not guilty either of rape or of adding that drug to the whisky. What I am guilty of, in the eyes of Allah, is drinking alcohol, smoking hashish and fornicating. But I believe under the law, I am only guilty of smoking the hashish, and that is a misdemeanour, no?"

"OK, if you do not want to tell me the truth, we will leave it up to the judge to decide whether he believes you or not. You admit that you passed the night with the girl, you were caught in *flagrant délit* by reliable witnesses, so nothing to be denied. You also admit that you and she drunk the bottle of whisky together and that you both smoked the hashish. All that is clear and to your benefit but what you have not admitted is that you put the GHB in the bottle and then abused the girl while she was incapacitated and unable to resist you. And there lies the real issue: the premediated act of drugging and then raping the tourist girl. So I will give you one last opportunity to come clean. If you want my advice, the judge will be much more sympathetic with you if you cooperate with me now."

"Sir, I cannot confess to a lie. I am here in front of you and I admit to being ashamed to have acted in a manner that is an insult to my God. Yes, I smoked weed, yes, I drank alcohol, yes, I fornicated but no, I did not drug the girl and no, I did not rape her. Whatever you say, whatever you believe, whatever the judge may decide, I cannot add to my sins by admitting something I did not do, *saeadani ya Allah.*"

After that long and emotional interview, I was left alone in my cell for two days. Once the realism dawned that I was locked in a cell and accused of a heinous crime that could net me many years in prison, so the depression set in and I cursed myself for abandoning the pious path that I should have followed. Now, my biggest concern was to know what would happen next and my imagination ran wild. What actually did occur was nothing that I could have imagined.

Sometime in the late afternoon of my third day in the prison, a warden came to my cell and told me to follow him to an appointment with my lawyer (I had no idea that I had a lawyer but I supposed that the *Baye Fall* must have need of one quite frequently).

I was left sitting behind a table in an otherwise empty room with the exception of a pair of chairs that faced the table and were fixed to the floor.

The door opened and in walked two men, dressed in courtroom garb, wigs and all. They were followed into the room by my guard. The taller and obviously older of my two visitors told the guard "you will wait outside; this meeting retains client-lawyer privilege. We will knock when we have finished the interview." The guard nodded and left without a word.

Once we were alone in the room, the second of my visitors, my legal team I suppose, raised the wig, and it was Matar. His finger raised immediately to his lips to shush me.

We all sat down and my lawyer began to explain the situation and that it had been decided to get me out of prison. The Brotherhood had tried using its influence to get the case dropped but had received too much resistance from the detective inspector, the judge in charge of the case and especially the German Embassy. Since that route was blocked, they had decided to go with Plan B. This plan was simple (when said quickly!) and was to use the close resemblance between myself and Matar. Indeed, as my lawyer was explaining the plan to me so Matar was removing his over garments and wig and placing them on the table, mimicking me to do the same and then to start getting myself dressed in his clothes.

Five minutes later, Matar was wearing my prison clothes and sitting in my old seat with his head held tightly in his hands and sobbing. The lawyer beckoned to me to stand up and move behind him. A quick rap on the door and a shouted "guard, we are finished here." And we were moving through the door.

After thanking the guard for his help, the lawyer slipped him a five thousand CFA note and said "please give the young man fifteen minutes to dry his tears before you move him back to his cell. I would hate the other prisoners to see him in such an emotional state. Is that OK?"

"Thank you, sir. No problem," replied the guard.

We walked as rapidly as we could out of that prison with the lawyer keeping up a continual legal chatter to me about some fictional case and allowing me the occasional chance to reply yes or no. Immediately outside the prison gates stood a white Citroen C4 with tinted windows and green diplomatic number plates. The lawyer told me to get in the back and keep my head down while he climbed in front and drove rapidly away. We were soon on the N1 Highway heading towards the *Patte d'oie* roundabout and from there driving off the Dakar peninsular.

"Where are we going Mr Lawyer?" I asked.

"First to Touba, of course. We need to get you well away from the shit you have landed yourself in. And you can stop calling me 'Mr Lawyer', my name is Pape. The real lawyer should be arriving at the prison about now – he will be in for a big surprise!"

And indeed he was because when he arrived to see me, he was met by Matar who handed him his national identity card and declared that he had been tricked into remaining behind. Fifteen minutes later, an embarrassed prison service was obliged to release Mr Matar Fall who was accompanied out of the prison by the real lawyer.

You can believe me when I tell you that my reception in Touba was not gentle. I was called into a meeting room where sat my father, my old Imam and the Imam of the third biggest and most important mosque in Touba. I was not asked to speak, only listen, and these three most key men in my life progressively explained to me how I had brought shame first on my family, then on my school and finally on my religion and its servants. I was to be punished for my sins.

Naively given my young age, I imagined that their punishment would involve me working long hours in the fields or cleaning around the mosque or some other menial tasks. But no, since I was now an escaped criminal, the punishment these three men had decided for me was that I should be sent to Europe to earn money to repay my debt to the community. This debt started with the cost of getting me out of prison, continued with the expensive passage to Europe and finished with the initial cost of keeping me in my, as yet, unknown destination country before I could start earning and repaying.

Once arrived, if I survived the passage that is, I would meet up with an assigned team leader and be helped to settle in and begin working. I was destined to be a clando (a clandestine or illegal immigrant) and join the Brotherhood's European contingent who worked then (and still do) in an array of different jobs; none legal, all under the radar. The most conspicuous of this contingent are the street traders who work in and around local markets or tourist resorts and pester potential clients to buy their knock-off products. I am sure must people in Europe have been tempted by the low prices of the *genuine* fakes on sale of household names like Chanel, Hermès and Dior be they bags, sunglasses or fake leather belts.

I had heard stories that the more savvy and persuasive clandos could earn several thousand euros per month in the high season at coastal resorts in France, Italy and Spain. That sounded good on the surface, I agree, but from such a total, a good percentage would be skimmed off to be repatriated via the Hawala system back to Touba. Our version of national income tax, if you will. Another good percentage was to be retained by the clando community in country to pay for general costs like our accommodation, transport, food, medical bills, and the like, plus of course the payment of frequent police fines. Another part of any earnings was to be retained to repurchase the knock off products as items from our stock were sold down or confiscated by the police. Only a tiny percentage, perhaps five percent of earnings was ever destined for the clando's pocket. Now here I was about to become an active worker of the Brotherhood PLC in Europe.

My father remained in the room after the meeting, allowing the two Imams to leave before coming over to me with a crestfallen face and tears in his eyes. He managed to say, despite his tears, "stupid boy, my stupid boy. I love you so much but no one in the community is prepared to forgive you for the evil things that you got up to in Dakar. You have brought shame on your family and religion and have to be punished severely. I have managed to persuade the Imam of the mosque to agree that you will only need to work in Europe for ten years, after that we will find a way to bring you back. But for now, I ask you to make us proud in your endeavours in Europe. I can tell you that you are being sent to Spain."

I hugged my father tightly, fighting back my own tears, not for the punishment of exile in Europe – in truth, I was rather excited by the thought of that – but because for the first time in my life, my father had told me that he loved me.

As my father got up to leave, he turned and said "you will be leaving Touba in three days and you will be travelling with Mi-Mi Faye and with a certain Matar Fall. Yes, I thought that last one would bring a smile to your face. Please send your mother and me occasional letters to let us know how you are. Time will go quickly my son and you will be safe, *Inshallah*."

The following day Matar arrived from Dakar and he was brought into my room along with a young Wolof girl by the name of Mi-Mi (short for Maria). After Matar and I had exchanged hugs and said our welcomes and *na-ga-def* to the young girl who was destined to be our travel companion, a middle-aged man told us to sit down and began to provide clear instructions.

"You will each travel with passports," he then handed over brand new passports to each of us. "These are to get you through Mauritania, into Morocco and across to Rabat where you will meet up with the *passeurs* (human traffickers) who have been paid already to get you into Spain. The *passeurs* work for an international organisation linked to organised crime and with excellent relations with the Brotherhood. The group of *passeurs* in Morocco is headed by Spaniards and they are well known to us. For security reasons you will not be told either your leaving point in Morocco nor your landing point in Spain nor your ultimate destination once in that country. All that has been planned in advance with our local brothers. Once your departure date from Morocco has been fixed, you will lose the passports, either the *passeurs* will take them from you or, better still, you should burn them so as to leave no trace of your identities. Is that clear?"

We all nodded but Matar still asked the question "why do we not keep our passports and, once in Spain, use them to prove that we are all minors? Surely that would give us extra protection?" A good question, I thought.

The response was curt "because, on the basis of your passports, you would be instantly recognised as Senegalese. Then a database search by Interpol would throw up two things: first that Alioune, here, is an escaped criminal and second that the passports are fake. You burn them exactly as I have said. Am I clear?" We all nod our heads. "Now, here are three mobiles, each has a Senegalese SIM card and there is ten thousand CFA of credit preloaded on each one. These are not for calling home, they are not to browse the internet, they are purely to enable you to make contact once in Morocco with the *passeurs.* Their numbers are preloaded under 'mother' and 'uncle' on yours Mi-Mi, '*Papa*' and 'Rashida' on yours Matar, and '*Tata*' and '*Tonton*' on yours Alioune. Again, as soon as you have made contact with the *passeurs* and your passage from Morocco is fixed, you must burn the SIMs along with the passports. Clear?" We nod our heads in compliance. "New SIMs will be provided you in Spain as part of your welcome pack once you are safely arrived with the brothers." Finally, here is one hundred and twenty thousand CFA and six hundred US dollars for travel expenses that I have split into three different envelopes, one for each of you. That money is also to pay for food along the way but ensure that you keep considerable in reserve for unseen issues. I advise you to try to pay with CFA wherever possible and keep the dollars for those places that will not accept the CFA. I doubt many people in Morocco will want our Senegalese currency. Also it would be best to hide a good chunk securely away as you will be travelling with desperate and often dishonest people and will likely be stopped by officials who will try to rob you of your possessions. We are providing you with bags that have false bottoms; make use of those hiding places. Finally, the best way of remaining in Europe," and he looked directly at Mi-Mi, "is to give birth to a child there. *La Droit de Sol* is a recognised route for a foreign child born on European soil to gain nationality of the birth country. Obviously the mother of a European national would not be repatriated and, if paternity can be proven, neither would the father. Up to you Mi-Mi who of these two you choose as the father."

That last bit was a bit of a shocker and caused Matar and me to exchange embarrassed smiles while Mi-Mi looked down at her hands.

PART 2
OUT OF AFRICA

Early the following morning, immediately after finishing *Fajr* prayers, the three of us climbed into the rear of a bush taxis, an ancient Peugeot 504. The driver's seat was occupied by a bearded brother and the front passenger seat was shared by two slim young men who I guessed were either of the *Peuls* or *Toucouleurs* tribes. Our first destination was the outskirts of Saint-Louis where we arrived five hours later, dropping the occupants of the front seat. Our driver then said that one of us should move to the front and that allowed Mi-Mi to leave her rather squashed position between us on the backseat and move to the front.

After filling up with fuel, we travelled a further hour, heading north-east until we reached the little town of Ross Béthio where we stopped for a plate of food and to use the toilets. Within twenty minutes we were off again, always heading north-east through the semi-desert landscape of this part of Senegal. Finally, we started to see irrigated fields and signs indicating 'Richard Toll', 'Rosso' and 'Mauritania'. For no obvious reason, our taxi suddenly left the tarmac road and followed a small dirt track that passed through field after field of tomatoes until, finally, we arrived at the banks of the River Senegal. A small rowing boat was awaiting us and this quickly transferred us across the narrow stretch of water to the far bank where another bush taxi awaited, this time driven by a Mauritanian Arab. The taxi already contained three other passengers so that counting the driver, we were now seven: Mi-Mi making the fourth in the back and Matar and me squashed in the front next to the driver. But then bush taxis are always squashed, that is the only way that the drivers can make any profit. Once our *as-salaam alykum* were spoken and returned by the other passengers, we each handed over five thousand CFA to the driver and the taxi pulled away and headed north along a dirt track road.

The next few days seemed to go by in a blur. We always headed north, tended to avoid the larger towns like Nouakchott and stopped only to fill up with diesel, eat or pass the night, sleeping under the stars. 'Comfort' stops were few and far between although the hot, dry climate that we experienced, made the need for a pee much less pressing than usual. The food we were able to buy at small roadside stops was either half baguettes containing a few chunks of fried goat meat and onions or small amounts of rice with slivers of dried Yaabooy fish.

We made little conversation with the other passengers; travelling clandestinely as we were, we understood that it was better to say too little rather than too much. Another issue was that the other passengers, all three Mauritanian Arabs, did not appear to speak Wolof and only a little French so thankfully, they were pretty much incapable of quizzing us about our reasons for travelling or any of our future plans.

At midday on day four in Mauritania, we saw a strange flag flying above a few low rise buildings. "This is where I will leave you," said our driver in rather more fluent French than we had heard him speak throughout the trip, "the border with the Moroccan-controlled Western Sahara lies at those buildings. Up to you if you make your entry to the territory official or if you decide to travel across country and enter the Western Sahara clandestinely away from the border post."

What to do? I was not ready to have to make such a decision. Fortunately, Mi-Mi was!

"Let's travel as officially as we can," she stated. "I know that Senegalese do not need a visa to enter Morocco. The border police should give us a ninety-day stamp for Morocco and their occupied territories in Western Sahara. That should easily be enough time to get to Rabat. If the border guards want to know why we are travelling on this route, we should all say that we are students and so want to travel through Morocco as cheaply as possible."

Well, we did exactly as Mi-Mi had said and passed through the checkpoint with only a few minutes' delay as a guard checked our bags nonchalantly and undertook some saucy banter with Mi-Mi who replied in kind. That young girl went up in my esteem and I started to see her in more of a baby-making light!

Just outside the border building stood two taxis and we managed to get three places in the one that was headed towards the desert town of Semara and from there on to Haouzza. But the downside was that we were obliged to hand over eight thousand CFA each for the pleasure of travelling in a fully laden and extremely ancient Toyota Corolla that appeared to limp along the desert trails rather than drive smoothly along as we had hoped. But no good moaning. Our journey again took us due north and we passed through the driest land that I have ever witnessed, not a blade of grass in sight, let alone a bush or tree. Only massive sand dunes as far as we could see from the taxi. Nonetheless, we did pass several camel trains laden with baggage that were clearly going towards the Moroccan border but with what cargo, we had no idea. On occasions our elderly vehicle got bogged down in sand drifts and we were all obliged to get out and push and, on one or two occasions, even dig down into the sand so the driver could slide a pair of sand ladders under the front driving wheels to allow our escape from the almost liquid dust. No matter, we made what seemed good progress because within three days of leaving the border crossing with Mauritania, the driver told us that we were within a morning's travel of the real Moroccan border. That is when our luck changed.

The first indication that something was amiss was when we saw a small plume of dust rapidly approaching us from the north-east; indicating the arrival of a fast moving vehicle. Our driver warned us that we should prepare for the worst for these were *Polisario*; but that meant nothing to me or the other passengers in the car. We soon found out as an open-back, four-wheel drive Toyota vehicle flying a complex flag of black, red, white and green enclosing a star and a sickle moon drove across the front of our taxi, which had sensibly stopped. The back of the vehicle plus the cab contained several armed occupants, and all had their rifles pointed menacingly in our direction. Three of the terrorists (as we designated them in our minds) climbed down from the rear of their vehicle and began to shout at everyone in the taxi while gesticulating with their rifles. While their words were in a language unknown to us three Senegalese, their gesticulations made it abundantly clear that we should climb out of the car and lie on the ground. One of the other passengers in the car, a rather elderly Mauritanian gentleman with only a couple of teeth evident at the front of his mouth, began to protest. A rifle butt thrust and one less tooth soon convinced him, and the rest of us too, that protest was not an option, and we all laid down in the sand.

One of the armed group went to the rear of our taxi and started to pull bags out of the boot and asked us one by one to identify our own bag. Then he started to riffle through them. The first bag belonged to a young Arabic-looking man and it appeared that the gunman was not happy with his haul. He asked in his language and then in very poor French "where is your money?" to which the young man replied that he had none. Wrong answer as a rifle butt hit him on the temple and he was out cold. Another of the Polisario group then went through his pockets and discovered a small wad of local money and put it into his back pocket. My bag was selected next and I prayed that my emergency stash was well hidden in the false bottom of my bag. The rifleman repeated his question, this time directed at me "where is your money?" and I held out a small wad of CFA notes that I removed from my back pocket; some seven thousand in total. Next was the turn of a young Mauritanian girl who was travelling with the unconscious man. She told the riflemen that they had taken all their money from her husband.

One replied with a lascivious sneer "we are not after money this time my little chicken!"

I felt Mi-Mi stiffen beside me, and I was immediately worried for her. As it happened, her bag was searched next and they found six five-hundred CFA notes. Also, without being asked, she handed over a further five thousand CFA note from her pocket. Finally, it was Matar's turn and they found a few notes in his bag to which he added a few extra from his pockets making a total of eight thousand CFA. Our stock of money had just been reduced by twenty-three thousand CFA, a relative fortune for the three of us, although we still had managed to retain a tidy sum of CFA and all of our US dollars secreted away in our bags.

While I was still silently congratulating my little group for not losing all our cash reserves, one of the gunmen grabbed the Mauritanian lady's hand and said "come with me little chicken." Another went over to Mi-Mi and took her hand, tugging against her feeble resistance.

The two girls were taken by several of the men behind their Toyota pickup while one stayed in front of us with his gun pointed at our group. We were completely defenceless and unable to help the poor ladies. We soon heard the screams of one of the ladies and then their crying and whimpering went on for long minutes. Finally, the women were led back to us. Both had blood stains on the fronts of their dresses and tear stains down their faces.

Our taxi driver motioned to all of us to get back into the car, threw our bags in the boot and drove away as rapidly as his old car would travel over the sand.

I reached across to Mi-Mi and held her hand. She lay her head on my shoulder and her tears flowed on to my shirt. "Are you OK? Is there anything I can do?"

"I'm OK Alioune. I'm crying for the other lady who was raped four times. My luck was in because my blood period started to flow only this morning. Those men saw the blood-soaked cloth wodge as soon as they pulled down my dress and knickers. None of them wanted me then!"

Ooph, I thought.

I then turned my attention to the old man who had a cloth held to his mouth and asked him in French if he was OK. He turned his head to me and showed me the bloody gap in his already almost toothless mouth and then told me with a small, bitter laugh that the gunmen had forgotten to go through his pockets. None of us tried to make any conversation with the Arabic couple in the front seat. The man was only now coming around and he would soon be faced with dealing with a wife raped several times by these self-appointed 'Freedom-fighters'.

We eventually arrived at two in the afternoon at the border crossing between Western Sahara and Morocco near to the village of Abteih. Here we said goodbye to our driver and fellow passengers, leaving the young Arabic couple and the elderly gentleman to speak with the local police and seek out some medical help for their wounds and trauma. With the border police distracted by the other travellers, Mi-Mi, Matar and I were able to pass relatively easily through the small border checkpoint. Outside, awaiting customers, was a vehicle that the driver said was going to Rabat via several intermediary towns, including Casablanca. Once another passenger had also paid his fare and taken the front seat next to the driver, we were soon travelling along the *Route Nationale 14* seeing indications for Tan-Tan. The taxi driver told us, in passable French, that at Tan-Tan we would pick up the excellent *Route Nationale* 1 that would take us northwards before we switched on to the *autoroute*. Once on the *autoroute*, we would rapidly reach Casablanca and then on to Rabat. Our final destination, at least of this leg of the journey, lay *only* some one thousand kilometres distant from our actual spot. Arrival time was predicted for midday tomorrow.

Snuggled as all three of us were in the back seats, Matar whispered to me in Wolof that we should soon start to check our phones for the presence of a signal. If we could get one this far outside of the large towns, it would be sensible to call '*ton-ton*' about our arrival tomorrow; perhaps at one of the next comfort stops. Mi-Mi and I understood what he meant and we decided that Matar should be the first to switch on his phone while we conserved our batteries for later.

The trip went smoothly with an occasional stop for the toilet or to fill up with fuel. Each time we stopped, Matar switched on his phone ... but no signal was available. Our driver, seeing this gesture, advised that we would be lucky to obtain even a single bar until we got significantly closer to Casablanca, and so it proved.

Finally, we arrived on the outskirts of Casablanca and, true to the driver's words, Matar obtained three bars on his phone. We left the motorway and stopped at a railway station where our fellow passenger alighted and disappeared rapidly through the gates of the station. Matar took this opportunity to switch on his phone and make a call to 'Rashida'. After three rings, a female voice responded with an *as-salaam alykum*. Matar spoke rapidly in French and without interruption, telling the lady that we were the three Senegalese from Touba, that we had arrived on the outskirts of Casablanca and would be arriving in Rabat in about ninety minutes. Her short response was to instruct us to get dropped off at Rabat Agdal station and when approached by a young white-skinned man to use a single word 'Touba' to identify ourselves.

Once we were again underway, we asked our driver if he could drop us at the Agdal station as we needed to continue our journey from there on the train. He replied with a smile, telling us that he was grateful because Agdal, being towards the southern outskirts of the capital, would save him an unwanted trip into the town centre to drop us off there.

The three of us descended the taxi at Agdal and were all surprised at the development of this part of the city with smart buildings and hotels and, in the distance, a view across the sea. We stood in a huddle outside one of the station entrances with our bags on the floor in front of us and tried not to look too obviously like foreigners. But of course, being three very dark-skinned individuals, as most people from the Peanut Basin tend to be, I am sure we did rather stick out like sore thumbs among the Arab, Berber and *Métisse* population of Rabat. After a thirty-minute wait, a young white-skinned man came along our pavement, stopped in front of us but facing away while looking at and apparently speaking into his phone. I said a single word "Touba" and he immediately replied out loud but as if talking into his phone that we should wait ten seconds and then follow behind him.

We allowed him to advance a dozen or so metres before we picked up our bags and trailed after him, ensuring that we always kept a small gap between us. Fully fifteen minutes later, after we had turned left and right and, it seemed to me walked in an odd-shaped circle, we saw a sign for the university. He turned into a side gate of the campus that led to a carpark and walked behind several parked vehicles before arriving at a smart Citroën Berlingo with blacked out windows at the rear. There was another pale-skinned person behind the steering wheel who remained seated and said nothing while our guide opened the rear door and told us to get in. Next, he asked for our passports and placed them in a plastic bag and then for our phones. I instinctively handed mine over, Matar cautiously removed his from his pocket and reluctantly handed it over while Mi-Mi said that only the men had been given phones. No further questions were asked of her. Our contact removed the SIM cards from the two phones and these were also placed into the plastic bag while the two phones were handed back to us. He then took three pairs of eye-shades from his jacket pocket and told us to put them on and to keep them on until we were told that we could remove them. He stressed to us that the shades were protection both for his organisation and for us. If any of us knew where we were being taken to stay until our crossing could be arranged, his boss would be obliged to kill us all. We did not need any further persuading to make sure that our eyeshades were fixed correctly in place!

The car set off immediately from the carpark and I remembered that my watch had read almost 2 pm before the blinds came down and stygian darkness prevailed. I also remembered thinking that we would likely be in for perhaps a thirty-minute drive until we got out of the city and arrived at our destination for today; but no such luck. We travelled for ages, for several hours I guessed, and while we could not see, our ears were still working and I noted that after the first hour or so, the road sounds diminished until we appeared to be travelling at a fair lick while the only noise was the honking of an occasional car horn. At some point, I must have fallen asleep because the next thing I knew was that Matar was gently nudging me awake and reminding me to keep my eyeshades in place.

The car had apparently arrived at its destination as we were helped out of the vehicle, our legs being very shaky after such a long drive, and led by the hand along a gravelly path that followed an uphill slope. Finally, we told that we could remove our eyeshades and, after our eyes adjusted themselves to the change in light intensity, we were able to see that we had been brought to a dimly lit depression in the ground; not quite a cave but a large sideways hole in the rock face. Looking around in the half-light thrown by two hurricane lamps near the entrance, I could see several shapes, other people, lying or sitting in the shadows. More clando refugees, I guessed.

I knew instantly that we were close to the sea – not surprising, I suppose, since we would have to cross the sea to arrive in Spain – as the sound of the surf seemed to be magnified by the indented shape of our new lodgings. We were each given a piece of bread with a filling that tasted fishy; perhaps tinned sardines, I could not see sufficiently well to verify, plus a small bottle of water. We were instructed to eat, drink and try to get some sleep for very early the next morning we would be making the crossing to Spain.

One of our guides, for that is how I then considered them, indicated a wide foam rubber mattress with blankets very close and to the side of the depression's entrance. I moved to the far side of the mattress assuming that Matar would lie next to me, allowing Mi-Mi to have the little extra privacy afforded by the outside of the mattress. But no, instead she came to lie next to me on the mattress and whispered that she was afraid and would like to sleep close to me this evening. Matar then took the outside edge, closest to the depression's exit. The paraffin lamps were extinguished.

Despite having dozed on and off during the long trip from Rabat, I fell asleep instantly and it seemed immediately – but it was likely several hours later – that I heard shouts and lights flashing from all directions. I felt Mi-Mi stir next to me and begin to sit up but I instinctively placed my arm over her waist, holding her still and flat. Matar, as was his habit, did not stir an inch, although I knew he was awake on the other side of Mi-Mi. And it was not moving that saved the three of us because the other refugees panicked and rushed out of the cave and tried to run in all directions. We could see that they were being chased by men in dark clothes; coast guard, police or perhaps the Moroccan military, I did not know.

As our fellow refugees tried to run off, we heard the unmistakable sound of the Berlingo that had brought us here from Rabat start up and try to make its escape but no luck for the Spanish traffickers because their car was brought to a halt by a dark blue, four-wheel drive vehicle that crashed into its front left-side.

We continued to lie on the mattress until the scenes of panic outside and the shouting of the chased and their pursuers seemed to die down a little. Then, keeping very low to the floor, we slowly crept out of the depression, remembering to pick up our bags on the way and gently moved in the opposite direction from where the majority of refugees had run, to the East that is. Matar told us to follow him carefully and, at first, we continued to move very slowly, edging forward only a few metres at a time seeking out the sparse cover of bushes and tall grasses. When he judged that we had put a hundred or so metres between ourselves and the depression, he set off at a faster pace along a narrow path, certainly created and kept open by herds of domestic goats. The logic of taking that narrow trail meant that the police vehicles could not follow after us and so, after an hour of half running and half fast walking, we considered that we must be at least six or seven kilometres distant from the police at the depression. We took a five-minute break to catch our breaths and then, in whispered voices, chatted about what we should do next.

Mi-Mi reminded us that she still had her phone with its SIM card and so we could try later to call one of the two numbers of the *passeurs* and get their advice and perhaps assistance. As luck had it, we found that we always had one, occasionally two bars, of reception at different locations as we continued to walk. After a further hour or so of fast walking, Mi-Mi passed the phone to Matar and he dialled the number under the contact name of 'uncle'. The phone rang and rang but no one answered. We assumed that the number must have belonged to one of the two *passeurs* that we were with until they got caught this morning. He tried the only other number registered on the SIM, this time under 'mother'. The phone rang two times and then the same female voice as we had spoken to yesterday answered. Matar cut through the pleasantries and identified ourselves and then said that we had escaped and had gone east into the morning sun. She replied that we should not have kept this number and if she provided us help now, we must promise to destroy the SIM. Given the circumstances we found ourselves in, we had no other option but to agree.

"OK, you should know that the police captured everyone else and they are all being taken back to Rabat and will be dealt with there. They also caught the boatman who would have taken you to Spain and several of my colleagues in different towns in Morocco. All their equipment was confiscated, including the boat and the car. I am free because I am talking to you from Algiers and Europe is not very popular here in Algeria while Interpol has no sway in my country. Back in Rabat, the police will quiz our *passeurs* whether there were other migrants with them who escaped and they will certainly respond with a no. Hopefully they will be believed but since you were not pursued, I think you should be safe for the moment. However, we need to get you out of the country as rapidly as possible since now, without passports, you are completely illegal and must follow my instructions carefully if we are to get you across the Mediterranean into Europe."

"We are listening sister," replied Matar.

"OK, so I can now tell you that the place where the police raided was at the eastern side of the Al Hoceima National Park. You tell me that you have gone east and have been walking since the raid, so all morning, that's good. If you continue in an easterly direction and stay close to the coast, you will arrive at the Algerian border. It is only about one hundred or so kilometres from your present position. Now, listen carefully, you should follow road signs and head for the border at Zaouia Al Habria. When you get there, cross discretely to the Algerian side. There are plenty of tracks that herders use to go back and forth to their fields and traditional pastures, follow one of them across the border. Once on the Algerian side, make your way back to the taxi stand behind the Algerian side of the border post and look out for a green Renault Clio. It will be the only green Clio in the taxi stand, Algerian taxis are usually yellow and black. The driver will be waiting there every day from tomorrow until the end of the week during daylight hours. Tell the driver the single word of 'Touba' and he will then drive you right across Algeria until you get close to the border with Tunisia. We have boats there for regular crossings to Italy. Is that clear?"

Matar repeated the gist of her instructions and then said that all was clear but that he was surprised that we were going to Italy.

She replied "while we can no longer get you to Spain, we can help you make the crossing to Italy. Once there, your instructions are to make your way through to France via the transalpine route. Your eventual destination is now Chambery in Savoie but you should try to make contact with the Brotherhood in Italy who should be able to help with your transport through Italy and onwards into

France. Good luck and do not forget your promise to destroy this SIM card".

Immediately the call was over, Mi-Mi took the SIM card out of the phone and asked Matar for his cigarette lighter. The SIM was soon a small molten mass that she buried in a shallow hole with a rock placed on top.

What now? We had to travel over a hundred kilometres and had only a maximum of five days to make the journey. But, for once, better luck was with us. Soon after burning the SIM card, we heard the unmistakable sound of a vehicle moving across the rocky terrain, perhaps some hundred or so metres distant from us. The engine was then cut. Of course, being concerned that this might be the police, we moved cautiously through the rocky landscape, ever ready to hide ourselves quickly should that be necessary. We peeped carefully around a particularly large red boulder and could see, parked only some thirty metres away from us, a light brown four-wheel drive vehicle with 'Al Hoceima National Park' stencilled across the side in large black letters. Underneath in smaller print was the inscription 'Funded by the World Bank'.

Four Europeans or Americans got out of the vehicle as we watched from our vantage point. They removed notepads, binoculars and other instruments from the rear of the car and began to walk rapidly along a sinuous trail that took them up into the hills and likely across to the sea on the other side. A scientific mission to the national park, obviously.

"Let's borrow their car," suggested Matar.

"But how?" I replied.

Well, Matar had another skill that I had never known about: carjacker extraordinaire. After allowing the scientists about fifteen minutes to get well away from us, Matar walked across to a young sapling and broke a metre-long wand of green stem. This he pushed down into the seal around the base of the window on the driver's side, gave a sharp twist and, heh presto, the door was unlocked. He told us to get into the car and close our doors quietly while he disappeared under the dashboard. Only a minute later, the engine roared to life and some ninety seconds after arriving at the vehicle, we were already driving along the dirt road that led out of the national park ... and onwards to Algeria.

As we drove, Matar and I chatted about where he had learnt his carjacking skills while Mi-Mi sat in the rear of the car next to our bags that were piled one on top of the other. From the front of the car, we could vaguely hear Mi-Mi rustling paper but thought nothing of it. Eventually she said out loud "those kind scientists not only lent us their car but they also kindly provided our lunch, look!" And she held up four brown paper bags, each containing sandwiches and bottles of water. At that moment we all realised just how hungry and thirsty we were. Time for a picnic!

Well, we ticked off the hundred-odd kilometres in just short of three hours, meaning that we were more than half a day too early for our rendezvous with the driver of the green Clio. We decided that it would be better to try to sleep in the car before abandoning it for good. About a thousand metres away from the border post and hidden off the tarmac road, away from populous areas, we found a small track that led to a field surrounded by a makeshift fence; a perfect place to take a nap and hide up until dusk. As the afternoon sun began to descend towards the horizon, we left the car where it was and started our circuitous passage across the Morocco-Algerian border. We believed it better to leave the car well-hidden because we did not want it found too soon after having been stolen from the national park and now dumped close to the Algerian border. That would have been too much of a red flag for the Moroccan police and immigration service.

As the evening arrived, we saw lights start to go on in a northeasterly direction; we assumed, correctly, at the border post. Given that we had all night to get across the border, we decided to walk south for a couple of kilometres, and then turn east which should take us across the border and into Algeria. True to the word of our lady contact with the *passeur* organisation, we found several trails, really small footpaths, that went due east and away from the setting sun.

Once we considered that we must have crossed the border, we continued walking east assuming, again correctly, that we would eventually come across a paved road that would lead us back towards the border post. We followed this northwards looking for all the world what we were most certainly not: three African students heading to the frontier post so that we might cross the border into Morocco.

As luck would have it, the first set of lights we came across illuminated the taxi rank where, early in the morning, we should meet up with the green Clio. The rank also boasted a small restaurant and toilets and so we decided to take a chance and make use of a real toilet and running water for a quick wash before settling down to eat. We could not believe that it had been already a couple of weeks since we had washed and eaten properly. Apart from a few curious gazes, no one paid us much attention. It was pretty obvious that we were either awaiting the border to reopen in the morning so we could cross to Morocco or that we had recently arrived from that side and were now awaiting a bus or taxi in the morning. The restaurant offered hot food and we were able to enjoy a large dish of couscous, mutton and stewed vegetables, absolutely delicious. Our payment in dollars was well received while we kept our remaining CFA hidden away.

After we had finished eating and our table was being cleared by a kindly middle-aged lady, Mi-Mi asked her permission to stay in the restaurant as long as possible. Apparently this was a request she received frequently because she told us that would be no problem.

The night went slowly and uncomfortably on the hard bottomed restaurant chairs but finally we saw the sun begin to peek above the horizon and, at almost the same instant, a green Clio drove into a parking spot just outside the restaurant; perfect.

We said our *as-salaam alykum* to the driver with Matar remembering to add the word 'Touba', we were only then invited to climb in and the car drove off, direction the far northeast of the country.

The driver told us that the distance to our destination was around one thousand two hundred kilometres and that we would be making the trip over a two-day period. As usual, we would be avoiding the larger towns which would speed up our travel and reduce the chances of coming across a random police checkpoint. Long story short, two days later we arrived at our destination; blindfolded for the last couple of hours, of course.

On arrival, the blindfolds were removed and we found ourselves in what I can only describe as a small bustling village ... perhaps camp would be a better word as this village was surrounded by a high fence of razor wire and had a large, locked gate protected by armed guards.

Our car pulled up near to a prefabricated building and we were able to climb out and stretch our tired muscles. Through the door of the building emerged a pretty fair-skinned lady who came across and shook our hands saying "hello the Touba-three, what an adventure you have been on! My name is Rashida, *Tata* (auntie) or Mother, as you wish!" We joined her in laughing at the joke and all thanked her for her help, especially when we were stuck in Al Hoceima after our narrow escape from police capture.

The next six days went by in a blur as we prepared for the trip across the Mediterranean. Our camp was as busy as a small bus station with people arriving every few hours in minibuses or cars while we saw others leaving in the early evenings and found still more gone when we awoke in the mornings.

Matar and I shared our dormitory room with fourteen other men, some speaking Arabic and a little French, others English and a few seemed to speak only languages that we could not understand. As time passed we learnt that these were either Afghans or Pakistanis from tribal lands near to the Afghan border. A final group in the dormitory seemed, to our untrained eyes, to resemble the Pakistanis but they spoke a little English and always seemed to maintain a safe distance from the Pakistanis. These we found were Bangladeshis and we learnt that they had, until recently, been contract workers in Middle-Eastern countries, especially Qatar where they had been building football stadiums in readiness for the world cup of football.

Mi-Mi slept in a separate dormitory that housed women and a few infant children, some born on the trip to our camp and often of father unknown. We remembered the frightening incident with the Polisario freedom fighters in Morocco-occupied Western Sahara and felt real sympathy for these poor ladies. Our trip had been hard and at times frightening but we could not imagine just what these poor girls must have suffered to have arrived this far.

During our first day in the camp, all new arrivals, including us, were subjected individually to formal and harsh interviews; of almost criminal-like intensity. The first barrage of questions that we were each asked were invariably to confirm our correct identities and then to ensure that we had no means of formal identification on us. The 'rules' state that all *clandos* must travel to Europe in strict anonymity. This is a safety measure to prevent the European authorities from working backwards and first defining precise crossing routes and then tracing back to geo-locating holding and departure locations on the North African coast. If a *clando* was a minor, like me, or not too obviously over eighteen years old, we were instructed to state the fact if ever we were stopped by police or immigration officials in Europe. That would give us an extra layer of legal protection.

During the evenings we tried to communicate with the other clandos in our dormitory. Both Matar and I had a smattering of English from our stay on Gorée and interaction with a few British tourists or Anglophone Aid workers based in Dakar, but really a smattering that served only for us to identify the other dark-skinned people in our dormitory as coming from South Sudan and Somalia. Most of the Arabic speakers also had a few words of French and they hailed from North Africa, mostly Tunisia and Libya. We could understand almost nothing from the Afghans and Pakistanis and found them rather a frightening lot with their faces permanently unshaven, hair awry and cold expressions on their faces.

Of course, as is a favourite topic of men, we spoke about money and how much a crossing cost and how the money had been raised to undertake such an adventure. We learnt from the Bangladeshis that they had travelled to the Middle East as contract hires employed by crooked, state-controlled agencies based in the posh suburb of Gulshan-2 in the Bangladeshi capital of Dhaka. They had only realised the fate they had signed up for when they arrived in the Middle-East and their passports were confiscated and they were faced with bills of several thousand dollars for their outward air tickets, accommodation and food. For almost the first couple of years, their wages were confiscated as repayment for their debts. Their dreams of promised riches to be sent back to their families in Bangladesh were transformed into dread of many future years of slave labour. In reality, their debts were repaid after eighteen months after which they were able to slowly amass a few funds. We were told that redemption came in a strange form. It came thanks to a dynamic team from the World Labour Organisation based in Dhaka that, after long months of trying, were able to penetrate undercover the contract hire agencies and reveal their nefarious and illegal activities. The government was so embarrassed by the findings that it instructed its agencies to cancel all remaining debts.

In our dormitory, it was the Bangladeshis who paid the most for the trip to Italy – probably because they possessed the most cash. They also seemed to leave the most rapidly and be replaced by others *clandos*.

The Africans from the eastern side of the continent had experienced the greatest difficulty in getting a place in the camp. One who spoke much better English than the others, slowly explained to us that they had taken more than four years to get this far. Travelling to Algeria had been difficult and, on many occasions, they had been obliged to walk for several days at a time or hide in trucks moving between different towns along the coast. Nonetheless, within six months of leaving home they had arrived in Algeria. Their real problems then started for when they tried to make contact with the *passeurs* to try to get a place on a boat crossing to Europe, they possessed nowhere near sufficient funds to pay their passages. These young men hailed from incredibly poor countries and from incredibly poor families too. Numerous of the *passeurs* simply could not be bothered by people who could not pay the two or three thousand euros for their passage. But finally, they came across *passeurs* from the organisation that ran our camp. They were told the price of a crossing, pretty much the same as the other organisations demanded, but then that there was a possibility of earning money to pay for it. The talkative young man had spent almost the last four years working in a call centre that made 'cold-calls' to the UK and other Anglophone countries on behalf of shell companies purporting to sell double glazing, home insulation and dodgy private health insurances. As we translated into French the gist of his story, two of the Libyans told us that they had also worked in a call centre for the organisations that made the same calls, but in French, to random households in France and Belgium. They soon had Matar and me in tears as they repeated some of the abuse that they had received from some of the so-called civilised households in France who were fed-up of being disturbed by their cold calling, usually during mealtimes! Slowly we learnt that the others in the room with no suitable linguistic skills had also worked for the *passeur* organisation but on building sites on the outskirts of the larger cities in Algeria. Clearly our organisation was a dynamic conglomerate that fed on the dreams and misery of the most desperate of human beings.

At the end of our first week in the camp, the three of us, the Touba-three as everyone now referred to us, were called into a meeting room where we were faced by the pretty 'Rashida' and a large bearded Algerian. Rashida told us that, all going well, we would be leaving tomorrow morning at dawn. We would be twenty-six men, women and children making the crossing and would be heading in the direction of Salerno in Italy.

Mi-Mi, whose knowledge of geography was infinitely better than mine, asked what we thought a pertinent question of why we were not heading for Sicily or even Corsica since both the Italian and French islands were far closer to our present position than Salerno.

The bearded man laughed and replied "because you do not want to be met by the Mafia in Sicily and I will not mention the reception that you would receive from the Corsicans. The Corsicans like no one but other Corsicans, even the French from the mainland have a hard time there!"

The next morning, we were up and ready by five am and driven to the beach in several people-carriers. As we climbed out of our vehicles, we were each handed a bright red buoyancy jacket. Each person to make the crossing was allowed to take only one small bag on board. Our boat was awaiting us, bobbing up and down on little waves at the sea's edge. 'Oh my goodness, is that tiny blow-up rubber boat supposed to carry twenty-six of us across six hundred kilometres of the Mediterranean Sea?' I remembered asking myself.

Well, 'yes' was the clear answer as we were progressively loaded aboard. Eight male bums sat on the left side, eight on the right, six women, including Mi-Mi, plus two children sat on the two flimsy wooden seats that traversed the middle of the boat and the final two men at the very front.

The boat was powered by a small outboard motor affixed by two clamps to a wooden support at the back of the boat while four plastic oars lay on the floor. The drivers of two of our cars placed two boxes of bottled water on the floor next to the oars and then, without a word, gave the boat a hard push off the beach. Once we were a couple of metres out, the boatman started the motor and off we went on the next stage of our adventure.

Apart from several crossings on the ferry between Dakar and Gorée, I had never been on a boat; certainly nothing as flimsy as this one. I would imagine that no one on board had any idea just what a vast body of water is the Mediterranean but luckily the weather was clement.

The motor hummed away gently for the first couple of hours taking us far away from the coastline and, up to that point, I felt that this was quite an adventure. A few people were violently seasick, including one of the children who vomited over his mother and a box of water, but most of us were OK. After all the sea was as calm as a bathtub.

However, my sense of adventure suddenly came to a halt when the outboard motor first started to cough and then to splutter before finally cutting out completely.

The boatman addressed us all very calmly first in Arabic and then in French saying "we are out of fuel, but do not worry."

He then opened the lid of a small box that sat between his feet and pulled out what looked like a microphone and began to speak in French "Mayday, Mayday, this is the fishing boat Achilles out of Tunis. Any boats in the vicinity of (and he quoted a set of numbers that must have been our coordinates) please assist, over."

Two minutes later came the response "Fishing boat Achilles, this is the Action Warrior II rescue vessel, we can be with you in about an hour, over."

"Action Warrior II, God bless you, over." He then looked down the boat and said aloud, again in Arabic and then in French, "this is quite a normal situation. Action Warrior II has been awaiting our call and will be here soon. No need to worry. I would appreciate if anyone who speaks good English can translate my words to those who do not understand what I have just said."

One young man started to speak rapidly in English.

The next thing the boatman did was again to pick up his radio and this time to say "Achilles to Base, over."

The response of "Base to Achilles, over," was almost instantaneous.

"Achilles to Base, we have made contact with Action Warrior II and they will be here in around forty-five minutes. Pick-up requested, over."

"Pick-up confirmed in fifty minutes. *A bientôt mon cher*, over."

That exchange was a bit of a shock for me and, following on from the labour-for-passage that I had heard about from my dormitory mates, began to reveal even more of the nefarious and corrupt world of people trafficking that we had entered.

I was woken from my thoughts by a ship's whistle and, on looking up, saw a large and rather luxurious vessel approaching us at speed. Our boatman called out to all on board our flimsy rubber dinghy "that's Action Warrior II. They will take you on board for the reminder of your trip to Salerno."

We were soon alongside the larger vessel and a ladder dropped down the side. We were told to remain seated until called or the boat could lose its stability and people might fall into the sea. And, once on board the larger boat, we should throw our lifejackets back into the boat.

Matar and I, being on the side nearest the ship, were among the first to be told to climb the ladder. Within fifteen minutes, everyone except the boatman, who stayed in the dinghy, was safely onboard the Action Warrior II. We were greeted by a crew composed of several different nationalities, judging by their skin colours and the languages they spoke. As we were helped off the ladder and on to the deck, we were handed silver blankets, a bottle of water and a cupful of something that smelt delicious and tasted even better.

I noticed that my fellow refugees were being split into their different language groups. Thus I soon found myself with Matar, Mi-Mi and one other man as we were led to one side by a young, bearded white man wearing a t-shirt – just like all the other crew members – with a picture of our rescue boat on the front and 'Action Warrior II' written in large letters across the back. Surprisingly, the bearded man spoke to us in Wolof, and a very fluent Wolof too. Not the Wolof of the cities like Dakar, Kaolack and Thiès that has been bastardised by the addition of far too many French words and American expressions but the pure Wolof that we had learnt to speak as children in the villages of the Peanut Basin. To say that we were surprised would be an under-exaggeration! It turned out that he was an American named Geoff and had recently spent two years in the US Peace Corps in Senegal and his assignment had been to a tiny village close to the Gambian border. He was now a volunteer with the Action Warrior Association based out of Paris and trying to save as many refugees as possible.

He had just started to explain the process for our arrival in Salerno, when I heard another motor approaching. Looking over the guardrail I saw that a second speedboat had drawn alongside our inflatable and was handing over a canister of fuel to the boatman. Within five minutes, both boats were speeding back towards the shore. 'Odd', I thought.

Once the boats had left, I brought my full attention back to Geoff's words. That is until I noticed a stunning white woman moving from group to group. She was not stunning by any measure of beauty – especially for a young guy like me – but rather because, well, how she looked. Giving an age to white people is never easy for us Senegalese but I guessed that she must be well into her fifties, in fact pretty ancient. She was wearing the ubiquitous Action Warrior II t-shirt and someone should have pointed out to her that she had forgotten to put on her brassiere this morning for her melon-like breasts hung rather low inside her shirt. Also her head, or rather her hair, looked like it belonged to a skunk for she had rather scraggly jet black hair except in the middle where there was a long, wide grey streak.

Geoff, caught my stares and said "ah, you have seen our Parisian leader, the old Therese. She has a thing for young men, the younger the better, so unless you want to share her bed tonight, don't let her catch your eye!" and he burst out laughing. Curious I thought.

He went on to tell us that when we arrived in Salerno we would be detained in holding quarters for a few days until we could go through Italian processing, and that someone from the Action Warrior Association would be our translator with the authorities. He warned that the Italian population was becoming very anti-immigrant and, in response, the government was clamping down and would only allow immigrants into the country if they had a skill that the country needed or a sponsor in the country or if they could show that they intended to quit Italy and travel to another European state; preferably England. I mentioned that we were all minors (although in truth, Matar was getting close to leaving that category) but Geoff, quite logically asked if we could prove that? Well of course we could not.

Once all the new migrants had been spoken to by mentors like Geoff, we were shown where we would be able to sleep for the night; mostly on deck, and then allowed to mingle with the other potential immigrants. Not only was our boatload of twenty-six immigrants on board but many others and, as we found those with a common language to us, we came to realise how similar were our stories: leaving dry land early in the morning, an overloaded boat, too little fuel to get very far, distress call made and saved by the Action Warrior II. Yes, I agree, the situation gets odder still.

As I was looking over the guardrail at the incredible expanse of the deep blue Mediterranean Sea, I could make out the outline of land to the north-east; Sicily and the dreaded Mafia, I presumed. My calm daydreaming was broken by a hand touching my forearm and, on looking up, I saw that the famous Therese was leaning against the guardrail and in fact had moved so close to me that our hips were now touching, how embarrassing. I gave her a polite smile and said in French "thanks for saving us today."

To which she answered as brazenly as you like "you can thank me in cabin 3 tonight. Come by nine o'clock if you want to get through Italian Immigration." And off she walked.

I hurried over to Matar and Mi-Mi and explained what had just passed with Therese. I said to both "there is no way I would service an old dame like that, passage through immigration or not!" But, if the truth was known, I had rather fallen for Mi-Mi and could not imagine lying with another woman.

A randy Matar came to my rescue proclaiming "I will go in your place; she will not be able to tell the difference between the two of us."

And that is exactly what happened for at seven thirty the next morning, a yawning Matar reappeared saying that old or not, he had never passed a night quite like that! That was the good news. The less good was what he had been told by Therese in 'quieter moments' as he called them. She had warned that the Italian authorities were quite capable of rejecting most of the immigrants on board, even of sending them straight back to their starting points. While this was illegal under European law, so was the fact that we were entering on to European soil without the correct documentation. She had advised Matar that security at the holding quarters in Salerno, especially for the youngest immigrants, could be lax and that he should try to get away during the night, make his way north in Italy and from there across the border into France via the transalpine route. Apparently, immigrant acceptance was better in France but we still had a long way to go.

As the sun started to move higher in the sky, we began to see land again, and this time not the island of Sicily. This was mainland Italy and we were travelling up the western side of the boot with the port of Salerno getting ever closer.

We docked at around midday and the Action Warrior II was met by a veritable army of people. While there were a few dozen men and women in uniform, police or coastguards we presumed, there were dozens of civilian men and women, many looking very much like Therese while, as our boat started to tie up to the dock, cameras were flashing from all directions. It seems we had landed in a flurry of press and television.

We were marched off the boat in single file and guided towards a group of buildings surrounded by a high fence opened by a solid-looking gate. In front of the gate were set three tables each with a sign listing two or more languages. As we awaited our turn, I could see written at the top of each sign: Arabic on the first, English on the next while the last said French. Underneath each of these most common languages were written other languages: Italian, Farsi, Spanish and so on. Since there was not a trace of our maternal language Wolof on any of the signs, we moved naturally towards the French table.

When my turn for the table arrived, I found two people sitting on the far side. One of them, a young lady, asked me in heavily accented French if I had a passport or any other means of identity. I shrugged my shoulders in a no and then was asked for my name and date of birth. These I gave her and she wrote them down on a card. Next she asked from which country I had arrived. I first said Algeria, then Morocco and when she replied that she meant my country of origin, I finally said Senegal. She then wanted to know if I had any family in Italy or elsewhere in Europe; I replied in the negative.

She then turned to the man sitting next to her and said in Italian what sounded like 'juvenile'. He beckoned me to follow him and my seat was taken by Mi-Mi. The man led me through the gates and towards a uniformed young man. He repeated the word that sounded like juvenile and I was led down the side of the largest building, through an automatic gate and from there into a small single-story building. The door opened into a large room with two settees and a TV that was showing a music programme. Mi-Mi joined me five minutes later followed soon after by Matar. The Touba-three were back together. From the entire immigrant population of the Action Warrior, only one other person, a young man from Sudan, joined us in our building.

At around six pm, according to the clock above the TV, four boxes of pizza were delivered to the sitting room and we were shown a corridor off the sitting room and told to select our bedrooms for the night. The front door was then locked with us inside. At around nine pm we decided to try to get some sleep. As Mi-Mi entered the first bedroom, Matar whispered to her that we would look to leave at around four am and so not to lock her door. Matar and I took the room next to her while the Sudanese boy went into the third room.

I fell asleep immediately and it seemed only a few minutes later that Matar was gently waking me from my deep sleep. "Wake up Bro, time to try to get out of this place."

We went quietly into Mi-Mi's room and found her sitting on the side of the bed already fully dressed. Matar went over to her window, opened the latch and jumped out. I helped Mi-Mi through the window and lowered her into Matar's arms while I first passed out our bags and then followed through the window.

We went over to the fence and by the light of one of our mobiles looked for any weak points. We soon found a loose pole and within ten minutes we were outside the barrier and free. Great security at this place!

But now, on reflection, we were outside of an immigrant holding camp in Salerno from which we had just escaped and had absolutely no idea in which direction we should go. Step up sweet Mi-Mi and her interest in all things geography. She told us that while on board the Action Warrior II she had studied the maps that adorned the walls of the mess room and had seen that while Salerno is a rather small, discrete town and port, the neighbouring city of Naples appears to be massive and almost certainly would have a contingent of the Brotherhood either working in the local markets or in the hotel and restaurant trades. We agreed that we needed to find the Senegalese contingent and make future plans on the basis of what they could tell us; perhaps they might even provide some serious help. So, it was agreed: next stop Naples. But how to get there, especially since we had just passed a street sign that indicated the distance to Naples was over sixty kilometres; at least a couple of days' walking and, not to forget, we were escaped illegal immigrants and likely, in a few hours, to have the police searching for us.

After the suggestion of our Geography expert, Mi-Mi, to go to Naples, it was then the turn of our Transport expert, Matar to come up with the solution. He suggested that rather than walk away from the port area of Salerno, we should look out for lorries and vans that advertise that they are from Naples. Almost certainly they would not hang around Salerno overlong before going back to their home bases. Once we had agreed, Matar then suggested that we should follow the road signs to the lorry park that proved to be a five-minute walk in the general direction of the sea. We entered into the lorry park, careful to remain in the shadows, and agreed that Mi-Mi and I would stay hidden with our three bags while Matar sought out possible transport. Logically on his own he would be able to move around unseen better than with the three of us moving together.

Matar disappeared into the faint predawn light of the lorry park. He was later to tell us that he had seen several large lorries with addresses in Naples written in large letters across their containers but none was unlocked to allow us entry. Finally, he came across a small white van on the far side of the parking that had 'Parello Delivery Naples-Salerno' written across the side. He tried the concertina door at the back of the van and it moved up smoothly with barely a sound. Here was potential transport. He came back to collect us and we moved quickly through the carpark staying well in the shadows until we came to the small truck. Matar very gently lifted the door twenty centimetres or so and we helped Mi-Mi slide in, passing her our bags, followed by me and then Matar. From the inside he equally gently slid the back door closed. We snuggled together for warmth and all fell asleep.

My dreams were disturbed first by a sensation of motion, our van was slowly moving forward and then by voices. We heard one man speaking but I could only pick out the word of *'immigrati'* (so it seemed they might already be looking for us) and then another voice that responded *'nessuno'*. I held my breath until the first voice said 'OK *vai*' (sufficiently close to French to have had to meant 'go') followed by the second voice saying *'grazie'*.

A few moments later we began to pick up speed and to hear traffic hooting. Mi-Mi had estimated that it should take about an hour to get to Naples and went on to say that it would be better for us not to enter the port area because it would certainly be under tight security. Best therefore to leave the van once we had passed into the outskirts of Naples; perhaps at a convenient traffic light or junction.

Matar raised the rear door a fraction so that we could see out but no one else, pedestrian or driver, could see us inside and raise the warning. Traffic became heavier as we entered a built up area, which was certainly on the southern approach to Naples and, at a convenient moment when our truck stopped and there were no vehicles directly behind us, we slid out the door and on to the pavement.

We had arrived in Naples and I marvelled at the fact that in little more than four weeks I had escaped from prison in Senegal, travelled the whole length of Mauritania, Western Sahara and Morocco. Then driven across the entire width of Morocco and Algeria, been shipwrecked (even if it was a put up job) in the Mediterranean, rescued by a Paris-based Association, certainly in league with the traffickers, deposited in a holding camp in Salerno from which we escaped after a few hours and then stolen a ride to Naples. And all that at the tender age of sixteen! I wondered if our luck was going to hold out much longer.

But rather than reflecting too much on our luck, we decided that it was time for breakfast. We found a small café in a backstreet off a main thoroughfare and asked in French for coffees, baguettes, butter and jam. I proffered a twenty-dollar bill that the bartender took with a smile and returned us a ten-euro note and a few coins as change.

As we were chatting about our next steps, Matar suddenly rose from his chair and left at a jog out the door and across the road. We followed with our eyes and saw that he had stopped an African man and was talking to him. The man then shook his head and continued his walk down the road. On Matar's return to the table, he told us that he had asked the man in French if he knew where any Senegalese were based in the town. The man had shaken his head and muttered '*non capisco*'. But Matar's sudden movement out of the bar and then just as quick return had piqued the interest of the bar owner. He came across and asked if we had a problem and if he could be of service. We explained that we were students and trying to get in touch with any Senegalese who might live in Naples because we wanted to find a Senegalese restaurant for our lunch. He disappeared through a door at the back of his bar and returned a few moments later followed by an African wiping his hands on his apron. The barman kindly left us to chat with his worker.

"*Na-ga-def,*" greeted our compatriot, "I'm Mouhamadou Sarr, do you need some help."

After responding to his greeting and asking how he was too, we quickly explained our situation and said that we were trying to get in contact with any members of the Brotherhood who might be in Naples.

"Well, you have found me already," he laughed. "What do you need?"

My curiosity got the better of me and I could not help asking how he had arrived in Naples and why he was working in a bar. He told us that he had left Djourbel five years ago seeking his fortune in Italy. He had read a tourist article about Italy and liked what he had read and so decided to leave his home town and try his luck in Europe. He had managed to get to Tunisia but did not have the money to pay his passage across the sea. An Italian *passeur* had offered him a place on a boat but he would be obliged to work for a Mafia-linked enterprise and pay off the passage across the Mediterranean. He had been working for Mario, the bar owner, since arriving in Naples. In reality, Mario had paid his debt to the Mafia straightaway and Mouhamadou had then paid back half of his wages each month until the debt had been reimbursed, a couple of years ago. After living in the town for almost the entire five years, he had made friends with many of members of the Senegalese Brotherhood and he knew that several of them should be working around the local market today.

We received directions from Mouhamadou, thanked both him and Mario for their kindness and went off to find our brothers in the nearby market. We spotted three of them easily enough in the early morning sunlight harassing what looked already like very harassed market visitors! We stood back and took note – after all this was to be our work when we eventually arrived at our destination in Chambery.

When one of the three finally went back to their piles of bags, sunglasses and belts strewn on lengths of green material lying on the pavement, we approached him, made the requisite greetings and then introduced ourselves. We were surprised to find that he appeared to know already the story of our travels and tribulations. Proof, if proof was needed, that even in Naples, the Brotherhood's bush telegraph worked amazingly well. In turn, he told us that he had been living in Naples for two years but was still working of his indenture to the *passeur* organisation, based in Algiers.

"Only another year to go," he told us. Hearing his story, and earlier that of Mouhamadou, made us realise the '*luck*' we had in being sent to Europe and our costs covered by the elders of Touba. But of course, they would eventually get their 'pound of flesh' from us too.

Our new contact then pulled out his phone and speed dialled a number. When he heard *'ello*, he passed the phone to me and told me to take the call and give our names and story. I started off by saying that I was Alioune Diouf, and straight away the person at the other end cut me off by saying "the Touba-three strikes again, hello Alioune, Rashida here. Yup, still me pulling the strings from Algiers. How are you guys doing. Say hello to Matar and Mi-Mi. I can see by the phone number that you have made contact with your compatriots in Naples. Boy-oh-boy you have done really well to get there so quickly. Now we need to get you up to the far north of Italy and ready for your little stroll across the Alps. Pass me back your contact there as I want to have a chat with him. Goodbye, until later."

We handed the phone back and he took over the call. We could only hear his side of the conversation that was mostly composed of 'yes', 'OK', and a few other generalities. But when he finally hung up, he said "Mme Algiers requested that we get you as far north as possible so you may cross over into France. In three days' time we have a van travelling to Turin to pick up supplies of handbags and other sales items that are manufactured in various places in that city. You can stay with us for the three days and then travel with the van to Turin. The driver will be one of us three and we will drop you at a train station and you can get a train from Turin to the little town of Oulx, not far from the border with France. Once we are back at our lodgings this evening, we can give you more information on what to do in Oulx, who to contact there and eventually how to cross into France. That will be the hardest part of your journey so far."

'Ominous', we all thought.

For the rest of the day we stayed with our new contacts, watching them go about their work and trying to pick up a few tips that we might be able to use once we got to Chambery. Of course, not speaking Italian, we could not understand the banter but what we did note was the stubborn way that our compatriots did not let anyone seeming even vaguely interested get away without purchasing something, no matter how small and cheap.

On three occasions during the day we were obliged to help them fold up very quickly their green material with the sales items inside (ah, that's the reason they were laid out on lengths of material) and run off to hide from the town police or *polizia municipale*. Once the patrols had gone by, the lengths of material and goods were soon laid out and hassled shoppers hassled once again!

That evening we returned with our three compatriots. They possessed an old and very rusty Fiat 124 that we all crammed inside with the market goods and our bags going into the boot. The boot was so full that the driver, a certain Diallo (a most un-Brotherhood name being of Guinean origin), was obliged to leave it partially open and tied down with a length of elasticated rope.

We drove through some backstreets away from the port and the market and found ourselves travelling through tiny streets of high-rise and not particularly clean or appealing buildings. We eventually arrived at what looked like an abandoned apartment block. There was no proper entry door, just a wooden block covered with corrugated sheeting and, to our eyes, apparently fixed firmly in place. One of the Senegalese gave a sharp tap followed by a softer one and then a repeat of the sharp tap on the iron surface. Obviously a signal, for a full minute later we could hear bolts being retracted and the door grate on the ground as it was pulled open from the inside. This was where they lived and the person opening the door was a heavily pregnant young *Sererre* girl that told us her name was Aisha.

One of the men pushed the door back in place and bolted it while the other two beckoned to us to follow Aisha up the stairs. At the top of the stairs we entered a room with a table and a few chairs plus a very scraggly sofa. From the room we could see a balcony through an open door and immediately outside was a traditional stove burning pieces of smoky charcoal and on top of which bubbled a large pot of rice.

As Aisha finished the cooking, we were told that this squat was their home and they had been living here for a couple of years. None of them knew who really owned the apartment but at the end of every month, a fat, baby-faced Italian came and collected a cash payment of one hundred euros as rent. They had never had any trouble from the authorities and so assumed that the apartment was being 'looked after' by a Naples-based Mafia family. But it was never wise to ask too many questions.

They then went on to tell us about crossing into France. So far, we knew that we would be travelling to a train station on the outskirts of Turin with a van driven by one of our compatriots. We would then take a train to the little town of Oulx where we must make contact with a group called Action Italia run by French and Italians volunteers who were dedicated to helping illegal migrants cross from Italy to France. We were told that we would certainly find one or two volunteers standing around the train station in Oulx, and that we should look out for their t-shirt or tracksuit tops bearing their group's name. They will provide you with directions to their camp. When you arrive there, ask for Elena. She is our contact and has already helped many from the Brotherhood cross over into France. She will give you the proper walking boots and clothes that you will need to cross the Alpine pass into France. Do not be fooled by the warm weather of Naples. Where you will be going it will be colder than the ice box of a refrigerator.

Well, to cut our story a bit shorter, we travelled with the van to Turin, were dropped at the train station, exchanged some of our remaining dollars for euros at a Transferwise counter, bought three tickets to Oulx and, within the hour, we had arrived in that little town. As predicted by our friends from Naples, the first people we saw were wearing Action Italia tops. One was a girl who looked just like a younger version of Therese while the other was a long haired bearded guy who smelt none too fresh (but then I doubt we did either).

We greeted them in French but they replied in English obliging us to work together to provide a very ungrammatical response. After just a few minutes, they indicated, mostly by hand movements, the direction we should take: up the hill from the train station, turn left at the traffic lights, third right and then straight on to a large house with a closed gate. Ring the bell and say that Emilio and Alice had sent us from the station.

We duly arrived at the house and were allowed entrance by a large middle-aged man with a shaven head. Our request for Elena was greeted with a laugh and a loudly shouted '*Lena viens ma petite*'

A pretty young woman with hennaed hair and a stud in the side of her nose came to greet us. For Matar this was love at first sight and despite his black complexion, Mi-Mi and I would swear to this very day that he blushed before stammering (and Matar does not stammer) "*enchanté mademoiselle.*"

Sadly for Matar, and luckily for us, Elena was all business. She took us through the front door and into a side room where a number of other Africans from Nigeria were present and being kitted out with heavy looking boots, jeans and warm coats. Once they had finished in the room it was our turn to be kitted out. Now, strange as it might seem to Europeans, none of us had ever worn boots or heavy coats in our lives, and only occasionally had we tried to wear shoes or even a light jacket. Senegal weather obliges people to dress for summer, not the ice box of a refrigerator! So, when Elena asked our shoe size, we had absolutely no idea how to reply. Mi-Mi found the easy answer by handing over a flip-flop and Elena measured this against a boot, stating that she was size 40 but she would add on an extra size to allow for the thick socks we must wear in the mountains. My size was 43, so I was given a 44 while Matar, being my almost identical twin, proved to be exactly the same size. We were next given thick pullovers and jackets, then knitted pompom hats and gloves. Once kitted out, Elena took us to a room with three beds and told us that we could sleep there this night and that we should be ready to leave in the morning for the French border. She also warned us that when we leave our room for the evening meal, we should use the key to lock the door, even better not to leave any valuables behind.

The following morning at seven precisely, our door was knocked sharply and breakfast called. At the meal, a young man stood up and said first in English, then French and finally in Italian that the following people should be ready to leave in twenty minutes. We were on that list.

PART 3
THE TRANSALPINE ROUTE

Eight of us piled into a rather dented Fiat people carrier and left with the same young man driving. Twenty minutes later we started to see signs for the French border and the town of Clavière but thirty-five minutes after leaving Oulx, the car suddenly turned off the tarmac road and went up a steep gravel-surfaced road and into a forest of trees first with broad leaves and then as we continued to climb, the trees began to look more like the Casuarina trees that had been planted along much of the coastline of Senegal as a defence against wind erosion. I later learnt that these were in fact pine trees and used by Christians in their Christmas celebrations.

After an hour on the trail, going steadily higher, I saw snow for the first time in my life. The presence of snow seemed to coincide with the quasi absence of any trees, no more broadleaf and very few pines. Our driver called out that we had just risen above the treeline and we should soon get ready for our walk. A few minutes later he pulled the car over to the side of the trial, got out of the vehicle and opened the back. Matar, myself and an Asian man were given rucksacks to carry. Our driver rather surprised me for he started to remove his shoes and put on well-worn hiking boots and a thick jacket with Action Italia emblazoned across the back. He picked up the fourth rucksack and told us all to follow him. We made a strange group of nine with our white guide in the lead. Matar, myself and Mi-Mi followed in a first small group behind him, the Asian man and a young girl (his daughter we later learnt) was behind us and finally two men and a sharp-faced woman. The men rather resembled our old Bangladeshi roommates from Algiers but they did not reply to us (or perhaps did not want to) when we tried to speak to them in English.

We walked in relative silence for around two hours mostly following a well-worn trail, covered in a thin and patchy layer of snow, that went more up than down. As we climbed higher and the snow got deeper, I noticed that we all began to pant a little as we walked. The effect of altitude our guide informed us. When the sun had reached its zenith, we stopped and all stood around a lonely gnarled tree.

The guide opened his rucksack and took out three bags. The first he handed to us and told us "this contains three half baguettes filled with sardine paste. This filling had been selected for the 'Muslims who lived near the sea'," causing us to laugh at his humour. The second he gave to the silent group and told them "this filling is cheese for the 'Muslims from the mountains'." They took the bag with no response, not a smile, not even a thank you. The final bag he gave to the Asian man and his daughter, first removing a half baguette for himself and declared "this filling is of the finest Italian ham."

We ate, mostly in silence, and thirty minutes later our guide got to his feet and we moved off once more. We walked throughout a long afternoon, occasionally taking brief pauses so that the little girl could catch her breath or for comfort stops.

At seven pm, our guide found an enlarged clearing free of snow and told us that this is where we would stop for the night. He gathered up some dried grass and emptied pine cones from his pockets and laid them on the grass. Next he picked up small twigs and added these to the pile. He asked the men to go and look for any dried wood they could find. Matar, the Asian man and myself went off in different directions while the young girl went to sit with Mi-Mi. The other three from the mountains just sat and waited.

By the time we came back with armfuls of dead wood, our guide had a small fire burning and this was soon throwing out considerable warmth. He encircled the fire with large flat stones and laid a large metal pan across the tops of the stones. He scooped in snow from well away from the path and soon it had melted then started to bubble away. He added in a dozen clean but unpeeled potatoes from his rucksack and, ten minutes later threw in three brown cubes that reminded me of larger versions of the Magi cubes that my mother added to all her stews. However, soon after entering the boiling water, these cubes, as if by magic, began to swell and form long tendrils of meat; mincemeat no less. Our guide told us that these were the wonders of dehydrated food and, I confess that here on top of the mountain, our evening meal smelt delicious.

When cooked, we sat around the pot and each of us dug in with our spoons, except the Mountain-three with one of them mumbling something about halal. My attitude was to be grateful to Allah for getting us this far in safety and for providing such delicious smelling food, but I suppose you cannot please everyone ... and also that meant there was more food for the rest of us!

After finishing the mincemeat stew, the guide laid out a few apples, oranges and bananas and told us to help ourselves. Then it was time to try to get some sleep. The Asian dad and his daughter lay together and Mi-Mi covered them with a blanket from the rucksack I had carried. She then took another blanket and told me that she wanted to sleep close to me. Matar was about to wrap himself in a blanket but first offered two blankets to the Mountain-three and then lay on his side and was soon snoring gently. Our guide laid down close to Matar and seemed to fall asleep quickly too.

I had a little trouble getting to sleep for the close presence of sweet Mi-Mi had me thinking of a lot of things that did not include sleep, I'm sure you get my gist! But I guess I did nod off eventually for the next thing I knew was that the little Asian girl had let out a loud scream that woke everyone immediately.

We all sat up and, in the flickering light of the almost dead fire and of a half moon, saw one of the mountain men bending over the girl and holding a little knife towards her throat. I then saw the other man bend over our guide also holding a knife close to his throat.

The mountain woman suddenly found her tongue and told us that they were going to take all our valuables plus our boots and jackets and that we should start retracing the trail back to the vehicle.

Matar, never being a faint-hearted individual stood up and bellowed at the top of his voice which rather distracted the man holding the knife to the little girl's throat. His moment of distraction was just sufficient time for the quiet little Asian man to release a sidewinder kick to the temple of the mountain man and down he went with a thump, out like a light.

The second man raised his head in surprise and this nicely placed target was not going to be missed by Matar. He used his two fists like twin hammers to pound both sides of the second mountain man's head, knocking him over and certainly puncturing his eardrums in the process.

But the fight was not yet over for the mountain woman had what looked like a Swiss army knife in her hand with the corkscrew open. She advanced threateningly towards Mi-Mi who stood her ground and then, surprising us all, released a crotch kick with her booted right foot that caught the woman cleanly between the legs. She went down sobbing and lay on the ground trying to catch her breath.

Our guide withdrew three plastic ties from his rucksack, telling us that he had brought these to fix a tarpaulin if it had rained, but they would do nicely to immobilise our would-be assailants. He tied the wrists of the two unconscious men and then took the third tie and placed it first through the ties of the two men before linking it tightly around the woman's wrists. Next, he removed their boots and told the woman that he would leave them the Swiss army knife – he placed it forty or fifty metres away from them – and that if they worked together they should eventually be able to reach the knife and cut their bonds. We knew that would not be an easy task as the two men were still out cold and so that would slow them down for at least a couple of hours allowing us plenty of time to get well away from them. As we got ready to leave, he told the mountain woman that they should continue to follow the trail that would soon enter France and that he would leave their boots five kilometres along the trail. For them to have to walk so far without footwear would put even more distance between us and them.

The six of us walked off along the trail feeling in rather good humour as our adrenalin buzz was still active. We congratulated the little Asian man for that incredible kick and asked his name. He told us that he was called Nguyen Lee Tran while his daughter's name was Kham or gold and that they came from Hanoi in Vietnam. Matar laughingly wanted to know if he was not related to the famous Bruce of the same name and the nickname stuck for, from then on, we always called the little man 'Bruce'.

Next we turned to Mi-Mi and asked about that kick in the groin. She told us that she had once turned on the TV in her house and seen a game called rugby where the player had kicked the ball far into the sky with a very similar kick, a 'Gary Owen', no less the commentator had said. Then one of her brothers had come into the room and switched the TV over to an American wrestling programme and she had seen a lady wrestler make just that move on her opponent; so she had thought to give it a try! Finally, our guide turned to Matar and gave him a long hug, thanking him profusely for acting so decisively when there had been a knife at his throat.

After about an hour of brisk walking on a now downhill trajectory, our guide dropped the three pairs of boots in the middle of the path and said in a raised whisper "good riddance." He told us that the trio had been nothing but aggressive trouble from the day they turned up at the association house. One of the men was from Pakistan and the other from Afghanistan while the woman was from Iraq. During their stay of a week at the house, several items had gone missing including the Swiss army knife that belonged to one of the volunteers and some dress jewellery from Elena's room.

The day passed very much like the day before (but without the knife fight) except that on one occasion we could hear people talking in the distance and they appeared to be coming towards us. Our guide hushed us and then led us calmly and quietly off the trail and we all ducked down behind some thick bushes until the three hikers passed us by. As the guide said, they could have been a border patrol so always best to be careful. We slept in the open air again and, on awaking early, felt more refreshed and ready to head out of the mountains and down towards the valley where lay Briançon, close to our next staging point.

Our guide told us that Briançon was a rather special place since it was considered to be the highest city in France at over 1,300 metres of altitude but that we would not be entering that town. Further down the mountain we found a footpath sign with green arrows that indicated a village called Saint-Chaffrey and it was in that direction that our guide took us. After about an hour walking along a narrow trail, our guide pulled out his mobile phone and said that he had a good signal and, as his way of thanking us for saving his life during the Mountain-three attack would do us a favour not usually offered to the migrants that he guided into France. He made a call, speaking in French, and quickly recited the news of our arrival in France. He then asked for a contact number for the Brotherhood in Chambery, said *ciao* and cut the connection. He turned to us and said "Rashida says hi." Proving that young lady based in Algiers really did orchestrate things both for the *passeur* organisation and the Brotherhood. A few moments later, his telephone made a quaking sound, just like a duck, and he received the 'visiting card' for our contacts in Chambery.

His call was answered after five rings, just before it could switch to voicemail and, with the phone on speaker, he explained the situation and where we were. He was asked a single question to verify our identity 'what are the three people called?' To this question we all called out 'the Touba-three' and the message came back that a car would arrive at the church in Saint-Chaffrey in three hours time, just after one pm.

At this point our guide said that he must leave us and start to trek back to his car. He kept one of the rucksacks and we gave him some of the food and an extra couple of bottles of water that we were carrying. He received a big hug from the three of us and we wished him a speedy return home. Matar also stressed that he should take special care to avoid the Mountain-three whom he might well come across on the trail. Our guide laughed and said that he doubted they would be in much of a state to fight after the beating that Matar, Bruce and Mi-Mi had given them.

After he mentioned Bruce, I suddenly wondered what would become of him and his daughter. After all, once we got to Saint-Chaffrey, we would be saying goodbye. But Bruce explained that coincidentally his transport would also be waiting in Saint-Chaffrey and his destination was La Motte-Servolex, a small town very close to Chambery. He was to be met by his Vietnamese cousin who had a French *'carte de séjour'* and so, thanks to his residence card, lived legally in France. They planned to set up a Vietnamese cum Indo-chinese restaurant in the town.

Soon after our guide had turned back towards the alpine crossing to Italy, we came across another signpost indicating Saint-Chaffrey ... 10 km, so we should arrive at the church in good time. We hiked into the cute mountain village with wooden houses and steeply slop-ing roofs dominated by its church with the tallest steeple that I have ever seen, even higher than the Sacré Cœur Cathedral in Dakar.

We arrived fifteen minutes before our pickup time by the Broth-erhood while Bruce's cousin was already waiting for him. Now how did they arrange the pick up so punctually, the sly little guy must have had a phone with him the whole time. We said our goodbyes quickly, remembering that we were very much illegals in Europe, but promised to meet up again soon in Chambery. Their car drove carefully away from the church while we decided to wait just inside its door so as not to draw any attention from the small number of people who were still out in the streets; tourists most likely. After all this was lunchtime and no Frenchman worth his salt would be walk-ing around outside. No, they would all be eating a large meal in their homes or at the Chez Puy Bistro that we spotted from the church.

At half-past one a rather battered, dark grey Toyota pulled up outside the church and we could see, even from inside the church door, that this was a member of the Brotherhood, his woolly hat and scraggly beard was a dead giveaway. I went outside and introduced myself and, when he was satisfied that I was part of the Touba-three, indicated that we should put our bags and the two rucksacks in the car boot and then climb in. Matar and Mi-Mi walked quickly from the church and we were all soon sitting in the car and ready for the trip to Chambery.

Our journey went smoothly as we drove out of Saint-Chaffrey along a two lane country road before turning right and going up a steep, windy and narrow road with the road signs indicating Valloire before eventually we turned on to a most amazing road that our driver told us was the motorway that would take us straight to Chambery. Sitting as I was in the front seat, I could see that the speedometer of our car was indicating 130 kilometres per hour. I had never driven so fast in my entire life, even following my jailbreak of only a couple of months ago when my fake lawyer had not gone faster than ninety kilometres an hour. Well, at such a high speed, the distance to our destination rapidly diminished until finally we arrived at the end of the motorway. Our driver told Matar and Mi-Mi to sink down in their seats, just in case there were police at the tollgates, but we passed through without issue and were soon driving into the town of Chambery. The Touba-three had arrived and the next stage of our adventures would soon begin.

We have now been based in Chambery for the past six months. We live in a squat not far from the Elephants' Fountain and Matar and I work in the local markets of Chambery, Aix-les-Bains and Annecy. Sometimes we go out to small villages when there are suitable car boot sales and *vides greniers*. Mi-Mi stays at home and prepares food and does the housework, washing and ironing for our group of seven brothers. She finds moving around a little difficult now that she is six months pregnant. Yes, you guessed, that night on the walk across the Alps when I could not sleep, well our relationship did go a little further than I related earlier in our story.

By the way if you ever see us working the markets, don't be afraid to come up and say hello. Do ask if any of the brothers trying to sell you our genuine fake designer wear happens to be Matar or Alioune; you just never know.

And, very finally, if you have enjoyed reading about our adventures so far, look out for further stories that our friend and former guide from Action Italia, *Pierre-Antoine S. de Vrai,* loves to write and publish with Cœur de Rose Publishing.

Ciao les Savoyards.